PRAISE FOR MARK BRANDI

'A storyteller who understands the power of the words underneath the silences. A writer who respects that less is more, and lets the reader bring colour too. A novelist of the highest calibre. A modern great'
SAMUEL JOHNSON

'One of Australia's foremost purveyors of literary dread'
The Age

'Brandi is not afraid to take his time. He draws [his] characters fully and whether we like them or not we are invested in their lives and need to know their fate'
Saturday Paper

'One of the finest Australian crime writers working today'
Better Reading

'It is no easy task to snare a reader within a mere few sentences and then hold them, eyes glued to the page, shoulders increasingly tensed, as a near-exquisite sense of dread urges the reader onward to the final page where one can only hope for a sense of relief – and yet this is exactly what Brandi does so well'
Readings

PRAISE FOR *WIMMERA*

Winner, 2016 DEBUT DAGGER, UK Crime Writers' Association
Winner, 2018 DEBUT FICTION AWARD, Indie Book Awards
Shortlisted, 2018 BEST DEBUT CRIME, Ned Kelly Awards
Shortlisted, 2018 LITERARY FICTION BOOK OF THE
YEAR, Australian Book Industry Awards
Shortlisted, 2018 MATT RICHELL AWARD FOR NEW
WRITER OF THE YEAR, Australian Book Industry Awards

'The reader is in the hands of a master storyteller . . .
This is literary crime fiction at its best'
Books+Publishing

'Very little fiction is as emotionally true as this. *Wimmera* is a
dark and disturbing story from a substantial new talent'
Saturday Paper

'What makes *Wimmera* so effective, and original, is the pacing
and restraint'
Sydney Morning Herald

'Subtle and devastating.
The novel crackles with suspense and dread'
Australian Book Review

'*Wimmera* makes excellent use of atmospheric rural Australia to
weave a gothic story with a strongly rooted sense of place'
Herald Sun

PRAISE FOR *THE RIP*

Longlisted, 2019 BEST FICTION, Ned Kelly Awards
Longlisted, 2020 FICTION AWARD, Indie Book Awards

'*The Rip* pulled me into its unpredictable waters, and refused to
let go; authentic, heartfelt . . . and original'
SOFIE LAGUNA

'A superb book – beautifully conceived, masterfully executed.
A winner'
CHRIS HAMMER

'[an] accomplished second novel that certainly
live[s] up to the promise of the first'
Sydney Morning Herald

'stripped-back and intimate . . . there's no doubting the skill with
which Brandi ratchets up the tension'
Weekend Australian

'a fast-paced crime novel full of dread and suspense'
Herald Sun

'another tension builder'
Courier Mail

'What held me close in this novel was not the idea of a hidden
population of drifters and addicts, but the writer's reassurance
that dignity and small kindnesses have a place in that world'
JOCK SERONG

PRAISE FOR *THE OTHERS*

Shortlisted, 2022 BEST CRIME FICTION, Ned Kelly Awards

'A story that hinges on a masterful thread of sinister unease running throughout . . . bringing together genuinely beautiful writing with a plot that is unexpected and unsettling'
The Guardian

'*The Others* sees [Brandi] return to his turf as one of Australia's foremost purveyors of literary dread . . . An immaculately sustained mood piece'
The Age

'[Brandi's] boldest book to date'
Saturday Paper

'In Jacob, Brandi has created a memorable young narrator, and in *The Others* he has continued, with compassion and intelligence, to explore the place of the outsider in a world that is not always as safe or welcoming as we might hope'
Weekend Australian

'As intriguing as it is heart-rending. Brandi is skilled at turning a slow burn into a gripping read'
Daily Telegraph

'A sense of claustrophobia and foreboding envelops the reader, only tempered by the bright light of our narrator'
ABC Arts

PRAISE FOR *SOUTHERN AURORA*

Highly Commended, 2024 FICTION, Victorian Premier's
Literary Awards

'If you only read one Australian fiction book this year, let it be
this one. Brandi tore my heart into countless pieces, leaving me
with hopeful tears'
SAMUEL JOHNSON

'Evocative and authentic, Brandi has created a world filled with
equal parts hope and dread. *Southern Aurora* is a special book'
SARAH BAILEY

'Another quietly riveting, emotionally potent novel from
Mark Brandi'
The Age

'The master of small-town dread'
Canberra Times

'Heart-wrenching'
The Australian Women's Weekly

'Another page-turner'
Who Weekly

'Mark Brandi has delivered a protagonist that could well become
one of Australia's classic characters. There's a Mark Twain
innocence and inner wisdom to Jimmy, one far beyond most adults'
Weekend Australian

'Brandi's poignant and deceptively uncomplicated tale pulses with foreboding – but also hope'

Courier Mail

'Unforgettable and unsurpassable . . . Brandi's observations are breathtakingly original and his insights are astute. *Southern Aurora* tackles issues with a purity that's as rare as it is precious'

Better Reading

'A beautiful and deeply affecting book . . . Mark Brandi proves himself a master raconteur, in a work characterised by gentle humour, perceptiveness and kindness'

Living Arts Canberra

'A powerful and deeply moving portrayal of a sensitive, vulnerable boy battling against the odds for a happy life'

Brisbane Times

'Moving and well-crafted'

AU Review

Eden

MARK BRANDI

Eden is supported by the Australian Government through Creative Australia.

Published in Australia and New Zealand in 2025
by Hachette Australia
(an imprint of Hachette Australia Pty Limited)
Gadigal Country, Level 17, 207 Kent Street, Sydney, NSW 2000
www.hachette.com.au

Hachette Australia acknowledges and pays our respects to the past, present and future Traditional Owners and Custodians of Country throughout Australia and recognises the continuation of cultural, spiritual and educational practices of Aboriginal and Torres Strait Islander peoples. Our head office is located on the lands of the Gadigal people of the Eora Nation.

 A catalogue record for this book is available from the National Library of Australia

ISBN: 978 0 7336 4935 6 (paperback)

Cover design by Christabella Designs
Cover photographs courtesy of Zora Zhuang / iStock and Michelle Newnan / Arcangel
Author photograph courtesy of Georgia Dodds
Typeset in 12.3/19.7 pt Adobe Garamond Pro by Bookhouse, Sydney
Printed and bound in Australia by McPherson's Printing Group

 The paper this book is printed on is certified against the Forest Stewardship Council® Standards. McPherson's Printing Group holds FSC® chain of custody certification SA-COC-005379. FSC® promotes environmentally responsible, socially beneficial and economically viable management of the world's forests.

For Millie

Part One

One

The city never felt like home. But now, unknowable. Another country.

It's dusk when I arrive. I long for a shower, for bed. My right knee has settled into a deep throbbing pain, the sort which might linger.

The man behind the counter has a dark beard, trimmed too neat.

'Just you?' he says.

'Yep.'

'How long?'

I shrug. 'Couple of nights.'

The man nods. Taps something into a keyboard, stares at the screen.

'Fifty bucks a night. First night up front.'

'Shower?'

'One bathroom each floor. You gotta share it.'

I reach into my back pocket, take out my wallet. Inside is a thick wad of fifty-dollar notes, a few twenties, wrapped tight in a rubber band.

I peel off a fifty. The man eyes me.

'A few moths in there, by the looks.'

'Huh?'

'Forget it.'

The man reaches under the counter, places a sheet of paper on top.

Something seems to alter in his expression as he passes me the form. A quick shift in his gaze, left and right.

It's something I've learned to trust – the physical. Eyes, mouth, and skin. The flush of pink as blood pressure rises.

'Rules of the house,' he says. 'Sign down the bottom, then print your name underneath.'

I hesitate, hope the man doesn't notice.

Does he recognise me? He couldn't, could he?

I sign my name, pass back the page.

The man reaches again under the counter, this time for a length of thick steel pipe. It's maybe two feet long, black electrical tape around one end. He taps the wooden countertop.

'This is my friend, Hector. Hector enforces the rules, you got it?'

'Got it.'

He hands me a brass key attached to a blue plastic key ring.

'Room sixteen. Up the stairs and to the left. No smoking, right?'

'Right.'

I feel for my lucky charm, the rabbit's foot, in my jacket. I give it a squeeze.

The staircase is narrow, the steps irregular. Back inside, everything was ergonomic. Not many places to trip, only a few hanging points.

The carpet here is threadbare and acrid. The ceiling low, the light dim. To the right, there's a green illuminated FIRE EXIT sign above a padlocked door. At the end of the hallway, another door with a small window of mottled glass. Must be the bathroom.

On the right side of the hallway, near the bathroom, a door sits ajar. A wedge of grey light cuts across the carpet. To the left are rooms eighteen, seventeen, sixteen.

The key turns too easily in the lock, like someone has had a good crack at it. Maybe more than once. The door swings silently on its hinges.

Fading daylight filters in through the window, the yellowed blind pulled halfway down. The faint odour of stale piss. I reach around the doorframe and find the light switch.

The room is small, but bigger than my cell. There's a single bed in one corner, with part of the bedhead covering the window. I open the blind fully. The view faces the tall concrete wall of a high-rise carpark, a dark and narrow laneway below. A colonial-style wooden cupboard sits on the other side of the bed. On its door, a Geelong Football Club sticker. I can tell it's Gary Ablett, even with half his face torn off.

I picture a bedroom somewhere, some kid who worshipped Geelong. Gary Ablett, Billy Brownless, maybe Mark Bairstow. Rolled-up footy socks kicked around his room, so his mum and dad won't hear. The MCG, grand final day, a kick for goal after the siren.

Then in summer, endless games of backyard cricket with his best mate. One hand, one bounce. Over the fence is six and out.

I take out my wallet, put a couple of twenties in my front jeans pocket, then slide the wallet between the mattress and frame.

I sling my bag onto the bed, unzip it. I think about putting my clothes in the cupboard, decide against it.

In the end pocket of my bag, my toiletries. I empty out the plastic bag onto the bed. Disposable razor, can of shaving cream, bar of soap, toothbrush, toothpaste. I leave the razor and the shaving cream, put the rest back inside the plastic bag. I strip down to my undies and socks, put my t-shirt back on.

A faded blue towel hangs from a hook on the back of the door. I come close to sniffing it, decide against it. I drape it over my left shoulder. On the door, beneath where the towel hung, someone has scratched 'Snake 85'.

I go as quietly as I can down the hallway. There's music now, a tinny guitar solo, and it's coming from the room beside the bathroom. A whiff of cigarette smoke. The door is still ajar.

Inside the bathroom, I flick a switch and the exhaust fan whirrs to life. There's one shower, two toilets. One has the door shut, but not locked. The other door hangs askew off the lower hinge, the toilet cistern smeared with shit.

I open the shower cubicle, turn on the taps. The water flows strongly. It begins to steam, and I feel a deep sense of anticipation.

I strip completely now, look across and see my torso reflected in the mirror above the sink. My ribs protrude slightly. My skin almost green in the fluorescence.

The water is a little too hot at first, then cold, then near enough. I let the full strength hit my face, my neck, the top of my head. I slowly lather my body.

I watch the bubbles run down my belly, my dick, and down my legs. The foam swirls, swirls faster, then disappears down the drain.

I close my eyes. When the bathroom door opens, I don't hear it. A second later, the light goes out.

Two

I clutch blindly for the taps, turn off the shower. Rough breathing, a stifled cough. I sense movement in the darkness, footsteps. I press my weight against the cubicle door.

'Who's there?'

The light flickers back on, the exhaust fan with it.

'Sorry, mate. Just fucking with ya.'

A toilet door creaks open, then a loud stream of piss.

'Ah, that's better. The name's Len. What do they call you?'

I dry myself quickly.

'Tom.'

Len lets out a long fart.

'Scuse me. Jesus, where's me manners?'

The toilet flushes. I wait for Len to leave. He washes his hands for what feels like an age, then starts to whistle. Finally, I hear the creak of the bathroom door.

'Come say g'day,' he says. 'Once you're decent.'

•

The door is still ajar, but I knock twice. Dire Straits on the radio. 'Sultans of Swing'.

'Come in, mate. No need for formalities here.'

I push the door open. The room looks much like mine, but a little more homely. Len sits on a wooden chair beside a single bed. He's stout, full-bellied, in white jockey briefs and a blue singlet. An unlit cigarette dangles from his mouth. His hair is shaved to a bald scalp, his dark skin shiny and smooth. The flattened nose of a boxer.

Looks Maltese, maybe. Definitely southern European.

I shiver as a cool breeze filters through the window. It offers a better view than my room, facing across the road to a strip club and its flashing pink neon sign. Miss Vixen's. Two bouncers, maybe Islanders, stand outside the door with their arms crossed.

Len reaches across to his bedside table and takes the radio down a notch. He lifts a can of beer from under his chair and takes a swig, then gestures toward the bed.

'Pull up a pew.'

I sink down uncomfortably to the springs. On the wall are some faded family pics. A holiday trip fishing on a boat somewhere. Len doesn't seem to be in any of them, at least not in his current shape.

'Like what I've done with the place?'

He grins, smoke-stained teeth. He flicks open a gold zippo, lights his cigarette.

'Want one?'

'Nah. Gave up years ago.'

'Me too.' He takes a deep drag. 'Beer then?'

'If you've got a spare one.'

'Is there such a thing?'

Beside his cupboard, there's a small bar fridge. He reaches inside, passes me a can.

'Thanks.'

I crack the top, take a drink. It's cold and bitter. Len helps himself to another.

'So much choice nowadays,' he says. 'Not like the old days. It was all just CUB back then, Tooheys in some places. Now we got all these weird labels. Goat rooting, get a yak up your arse, who the fuck knows.'

I nod, take another sip.

'So, what brings you to this shithole?'

I shrug. 'Just got out.'

'No shit. Not many come here for a holiday, ya know. Don't you have any family?'

I shake my head. 'Dad died when I was a kid, Mum while I was inside. No brothers or sisters.'

'Shit. Sorry, mate. About your mum, I mean. That's the fucken pits.'

Len reaches over, turns up the radio a touch.

'Love this song,' he says. 'That Annie Lennox was some pretty fucking hot stuff, don't ya think? I love birds with short hair like that. What a voice.'

'You been here a while?'

Len nods, takes a drag of his cigarette. 'Few years. I get a special weekly rate of fuck-all in exchange for being the local dogsbody. Do some odd jobs for that cunt downstairs. For his old man, really, but he carked it a few months back. That little shit will sell the place to developers soon enough, then I'll be out on my arse.'

I finish my beer. I'd love another one.

'So, the obvious question,' he says. 'What were you in for?'

The aluminium pings in my hand.

'Does it matter?'

'Something serious then?'

'Kinda.'

'Not some fucken rock spider, are ya?'

I shake my head. 'Accessory to murder. For helping out a mate.'

Len raises his eyebrows. 'Must've been some mate.'

'He was.'

'What happened?'

'Shit happened.'

'You're quite the talker, aren't ya?'

'I'll tell you about it some other time.'

'Whatever. You want another?'

'Yeah, but I'll pay you back.'

He butts out his cigarette, shakes his head. 'Another fucken freeloader. Just grab it yourself.'

I open the fridge. Inside there's a block of tasty cheese and a pack of white bread. I haven't eaten anything since breakfast.

'Beers are down the bottom,' he says. 'In the little crisper there. The fridge is pretty much fucked, so it's the coldest spot.'

I go back to the bed, crack the can.

'What about you?' I say.

'What about me?'

'What were you inside for?'

Len takes a big swig of his can, lets out a burp.

'Depends who's asking.'

I shrug. 'Just making conversation.'

'Yeah, right. It was years ago, when I was working out on the boats. I was a merchant seaman. Do you know what that is?'

'Sort of.'

'You go from ship to ship, job to job. Not much money in it, but it got me away from home. When I was a teenager, I mean. The old man was a bit of a rogue. When he wasn't in jail, he liked to smack us kids around, Mum too. It got me away from him, and it meant I got to see the world.'

I try to imagine Len as a teenager. Thinner, surely, but he seems the type who would've looked pretty much the same his whole life.

'Anyway, I got roped into an importation. Heroin, it was. Never touch the stuff meself, but one of the crew had this real clever plan. The dumb fuck reckoned it was bulletproof. Customs only check about one per cent of the containers, ya know. Plus, he said he'd paid off a couple of the wharfies, so it would all come through without a hitch. Set us up for life, he said.'

'What happened?'

He looks up at the photos. 'One of the wharfies got cold feet and squealed. The police came and got me in the middle of the night. SOG, it was. Those special ops blokes. "Sons of God", they like to call themselves. I put up a bit of a struggle, so they beat the living shit out of me. Put me in hospital for a week.'

'Jesus.'

'Yeah, Jesus alright. A lot of good that prick ever did me. Anyway, long story short, I did twelve years. All because I listened to that dumb cunt. So, I guess I was even dumber than him. Another beer?'

'I might turn in. I'm pretty knackered.'

I look again at the pictures on the wall, and I realise they probably aren't family shots. They're mostly taken out at sea. Little fishing boats, dinghies. Probably Len's recreation time amid the work on the ships. Some big fish too.

'Last one for me then,' Len says. He eases back into his chair.

I nod toward the photos. 'You miss it?'

'Sometimes. Miss the blokes, you know? They were like family. Wouldn't be up to it nowadays, of course. Too old, and I got the big C.'

'Cancer?'

'Yeah.'

'Shit. Sorry.'

He shrugs. 'It's my pancreas. A real fucker, it is. It's not going to be pretty, but something's gotta get you in the end, right?'

He lights another cigarette. I stand up, my head spinning.

'Thanks for the beer. I'll shout you back tomorrow.'

He nods. 'I'm always here.'

I head back to my room, staggering just slightly. First beer in nine years, on an empty stomach too.

I take my lucky charm out of my pocket, slide it between the mattress and frame. I reach further underneath for my wallet.

My breath catches in my throat.

My wallet.

It's gone.

Three

I open my eyes to the first light filtering through the window. For a second, I wonder where I am.

The blind flaps behind me, the air cool on my skin. I pull the sheet and blanket closer to my chin, curl myself sideways.

And for a brief and peaceful moment, I forget about my wallet.

I blink and stare at the wall.

Who could've taken it? Some boarder who had a copy of the key? Maybe the bloke who runs the place?

It was probably him. He saw inside my wallet, after all.

I sit up slowly, push the blanket away and swing my feet onto the floor. I lean back and pull at the blind. It doesn't retract. I try again, but it just goes further down.

I climb up and stand on the bed, the mattress sinking and squeaking under my weight. I reach up and roll the blind by hand. Grey light softly illuminates the room. I look outside, the concrete wall stares back. I need a piss something terrible.

In the hallway, in my undies, I move as quickly as I can. The bathroom door is open, but it's gloomy within. I leave the light switched off, remember the filthy toilet, and move to the other one. I piss silently against the ceramic.

•

The bearded man is at his post, eyes on the screen.

'Sleep okay?'

'Someone stole my wallet.'

'No shit?'

'No shit.'

He stares at me. 'Like I give a fuck.'

'You know who might have taken it?'

I study his face for any reaction, but he doesn't flinch.

'Who am I, Poirot? In this joint, it could've been anyone.'

'That's helpful.'

'Call the cops if you want. I'm sure they'll make it a high priority.'

'Can't you ask around? The other boarders, I mean?'

He narrows his eyes, reaches under the counter.

'I can check with Hector, if you like.'

'Forget it.'

He eyes me, then goes back to his screen.

'Do you have a map I can borrow? A Melways or something?'

He shakes his head. 'No-one uses those anymore.'

'Can you give me some directions then?'

He sighs. 'Where to?'

'Centrelink.'

'You've got no other cash then?'

'I'm good for it.'

'There's no rain cheques here, my friend.'

'I'll sort it.'

'You got paperwork? ID?'

'What for?'

'For Centrelink. They won't give you a cent otherwise.'

I remember a prison social worker saying something about getting things sorted a few months back. I should've listened. Should've done something about it.

The man scratches his beard, leans back in his chair.

'I think there's still one in the city. Let me have a look.'

He taps at the keyboard. I hear footsteps behind me. An old, painfully thin woman moves slowly and carefully down the stairs, gripping the banister.

'Morning, Philomena.'

The man says it without looking up from his screen.

'What's fucking good about it?'

'This might be it,' he says. 'Corner Exhibition and Bourke.'

He twists the monitor toward me. The old woman comes up slowly, leans over the counter.

'Stop stuffing around with pretty boy here and give me a few dollars, will ya?'

The man ignores her. She turns and stares at me with red-rimmed eyes. Her breath is rank.

'How about you then, fancy pants?'

'Sorry,' I say.

She shakes her head. 'Tight-arses, the both of youse.'

The man points to the screen.

'Once you're on Bourke, go straight up toward Parliament House, right? But pack up your room before you go. I'm feeling generous, so I'll let you leave your bag behind the counter, just for today.'

'Can't you just give me a few hours?'

The man shakes his head. 'What can I tell you? It's a cruel old world.'

•

I know I can't afford it, but my stomach aches.

'You want that as part of a value meal?'

Pale skin, pimples. Dark blue eyes and dyed black hair. Can't be more than sixteen, I'd guess. I suddenly feel a hundred years old.

'Value meal?'

She cocks an eyebrow. I notice a piercing hole. She must take it out for work.

'You get a hashbrown and a drink, plus the hotcakes. Nine dollars fifty.'

'Just the hotcakes and a coffee.'

'What kind?'

I look up at the menu. 'Cappuccino.'

'Regular milk?'

'Regular?'

She rolls her eyes. 'Regular, soy, skinny, or almond?'

'Regular.'

I pay and find a seat near the back, next to the toilets. The decor has changed, but the feel is much the same. The red and yellow less prominent, more subtle among timber and tiles. I remember someone telling me the colours were chosen especially because they spark your appetite. I can't remember who it was, or if it's true.

The pancakes aren't like I remember, but still good. The syrup is sticky and much too sweet, the pancakes too thick.

The ones Mum used to make were thin and salty with butter. Saturday mornings in front of the cartoons, just the two of us. Warm light through the window.

Those were always the best times.

•

I keep my eyes down, try to keep the sound out. I watch the footpath, street signs when needed. Avoid eye contact with those passing, cross the road on the red man.

Through the Bourke Street Mall, past competing buskers. Dark-skinned men in traditional outfits playing the pan flute, an extremely loud pop band over the road. Shoppers heading this way and that, noisy trams with bells ringing, smokers on steps. Traffic, shouting, music, construction. The endless crush of people. Exhaust fumes and bodies, food and decay.

I'd grown used to the quiet inside. The system, the repetition, the routine. Once you understood the rhythms, once you found your place, you just had to keep your head down. But even when you played by the rules, trouble could still find you.

There's an office block on one corner, a pub on another, a couple of shops. No Centrelink. I'm sure it's the place he said.

I look up to Parliament House, the huge stone pillars. There are two security guards near the top of the steps. I decide to ask them, think better of it. Then I change my mind.

I choose the most approachable one. He's young, olive-skinned, with dark eyes mostly hidden beneath the peak of his cap. He stands with his legs apart, arms crossed. Black leather gloves and a navy woollen coat. He watches me approach, clenches the muscles in his jaw.

'Help you, mate?'

Says it five steps before I get there.

'Just after some directions.'

He glances across at his partner, a grizzled-looking bloke, sun-damaged skin. He glances at the younger man, shakes his head.

'Not really our job,' the younger man says.

'Just looking for the Centrelink. It's supposed to be on the corner of Exhibition and Bourke, but there's just a pub.'

'Can't help you.'

I go back down the steps, eye the people walking past. Suits and the like. Most talking to each other, or on the phone. The rest with headphones in their ears.

Across the road I spot someone selling *The Big Issue*. He's standing at the entrance to an underground train station. The sign says Parliament. A steep flight of stairs disappears into the darkness underneath the street.

I cross the road.

'Hey, mate,' I say.

The seller turns and eyes me. Tight curls of an afro poking out from beneath his hat.

'Hey, brother.' He holds out the mag. 'Excellent edition, this one. Some great interviews.'

'Was just after some directions.'

He smiles. 'Always happy to help a customer.'

I reach into my pocket. Thirty dollars left. Have to make it stretch.

'How much?'

'Six bucks.'

I take out a tenner. The seller peels off a magazine from his stack, hands it to me. I roll up the magazine, push it into my back pocket.

'You know where the Centrelink is? I got told the corner of Exhibition and Bourke.'

The seller whistles.

'Man, there hasn't been a Centrelink in the city for as long as I can remember. They all got merged, meaning they mostly got closed. They're trying to push everyone online or onto the phone, which they never answer. Nearest one is over in Richmond. You can get the train down here.'

He points to the fluoro-lit underground realm of the station. I've got no desire to go down there.

He narrows his eyes. 'You just get out?'

'Is it that obvious?'

He smiles, yellow teeth.

'I been there, brother. You look lost. It's in your eyes, your clothes, everything.'

I look down at my jeans and shirt, my old boots.

'You saved much cash? From the work programs inside?'

'I did, but I got robbed.'

He shakes his head. 'Fuck, man, that stinks. Who did it?'

'Dunno. It was at the place I'm staying at. Could've been anyone.'

'Now what you gonna do?'

I shrug.

'Listen, you should be able to get a payment. One-off type thing. I heard one of the other sellers talking about it last week. But there's a million forms and queues at Centrelink. It'll fuck with your head. You got somewhere to crash in the meantime?'

I tell him about the hostel, that I'm short.

'Why'd you buy a magazine for?'

He hands back the cash, I pass him the mag.

'Keep it,' he says.

'You sure?'

'Yeah. But you want my advice?'

I nod.

'Go to the Salvos, just down Bourke Street here. They can get you in a shelter for a few nights.'

I glance down the street. 'Maybe.'

A well-dressed woman, navy business suit and red lipstick, stops in front of the seller.

'Hey, Rebecca,' he says.

'Hey, Jonah. Is that the latest?'

I spot the red sign of the Salvos in the next block down. A homeless shelter doesn't sound appealing.

I wait for Jonah to finish his transaction. I watch the easy exchange between them, like old friends from different worlds. She hands him a twenty.

'Keep the change,' she says. 'I'll see you next time.'

She turns and heads down the stairs. He puts the cash in his pocket.

'Seriously,' he says, 'try the Salvos. I don't go for the religious stuff, but they're good people.'

'Thanks for the tip. But I might just rough it for tonight. It'd be good to get out under the stars, at least until I get things sorted.'

He shakes his head.

'Suit yourself, brother. But watch your back. It can get real ugly out here.'

•

There are rows of red and white wine on the shelves, spirits behind the counter. The woman watches me with hard eyes.

'Help you with anything?'

'Just some beers.'

'Fridge down the back.'

I try to remember the brand Len was drinking. It had a red label, but it wasn't Melbourne. None of the beers in the fridge look like it, but I decide on Coopers. I pick up half-a-dozen, realise it's too expensive, decide to get two instead.

'Just those?' the woman says.

'Yep.'

She rings up the cost. The register opens, and I quickly eye the cash. A few fifties, more twenties.

Could I do it? Maybe get a knife or something? What if she puts up a fight?

I pay for the beers.

'Thanks,' I say.

The woman nods, eyes me warily.

•

The hostel man is still behind the counter. I think about complaining about his directions, decide not to.

'Can I grab my stuff?'

'No luck then?'

I don't answer. He reaches down, passes me my bag.

'Is Len around?'

'Do I look like his secretary?'

I sling my bag over my shoulder, head for the stairs.

'By the way, someone was here before. They were asking for you.'

I look back over my shoulder.

'Who?'

He shrugs. 'Didn't say. Some bloke with a limp. A real Keyser Söze type.'

'Keyser who?'

'Forget it.'

'What'd you tell him?'

'Told him you'd already left, which was pretty much accurate. Just thought you might wanna know.'

I slowly climb the stairs.

'Don't hang around too long, right? We're not a social club.'

Who would come looking for me? There's only one bloke I can think of.

•

It was almost three years ago.

He came to my cell with a violent reputation, worse temper. Ali the Turk, they called him. He'd done seven years for manslaughter, but was just a few months shy of parole. He was known for extreme paranoia and for holding grudges over nothing – a bad combo, whichever way you sliced it.

He was dealing smack when it happened. The gear got chucked over the fence into the yard once a fortnight, packed inside a tennis ball. Most of the screws turned a blind eye.

A random search of our cell got him pinched. He didn't see it coming. They found his stash, cuffed him.

He glared at me as they dragged him down the hall.

'You fucken dog. I'll get you for this, cunt. Inside or out.'

He got moved to Acacia Unit. Max security. He didn't get parole, last I heard. I also heard from another prisoner that he blamed me for it.

'You're all he talks about,' he said. 'Won't shut up. Reckons he'll torture you first, then chop you up into little pieces.'

As long as he stayed in Acacia Unit, separated from mainstream, I knew I was pretty safe. From him, at least.

He'd be out of prison now, though. Definitely.

He never had a limp, but maybe something happened in the years since. Still, he couldn't possibly know I was at the hostel. Unless he has a connection inside, someone who knew where I was headed.

I push the thought away.

•

Len stands in the doorway of his room, arms crossed. He eyes my bag.

'You've come to say goodbye?'

'Yeah. And I wanted to pay you back for those beers.'

I pass him the two cans in a brown paper bag.

'That's all?'

'That's all I drank.'

'What about the interest?'

'I'm pretty short. Someone robbed me last night.'

'Serious?'

'Yeah, they stole my wallet from my room. While I was here chatting with you.'

'How much?'

'About six hundred.'

He shakes his head. 'That's fucked, that is. But why the hell did you leave it there?'

'My room was locked. And I thought it was pretty well hidden.'

'Guess you won't make that mistake again. Listen, why don't you keep one for the road?'

He passes me a beer.

'You sure?'

'Yeah, I hate Coopers anyway. Tastes like piss. So, where you headed?'

I push the can into my back pocket. 'Reckon I'll rough it tonight, figure out the rest tomorrow.'

He nods. 'Fair enough. Spent a bit of time on the street meself after I got out. You want some advice?'

'Sure.'

'Don't hang around the city. You'll get rolled for sure.'

'I haven't got much worth stealing.'

'Even worse. They'll kick the shit out of you, just for wasting their time. Listen, this might sound a bit weird, but why don't you head up to the cemetery, the old one in Carlton. It gets locked up at night, so you won't get hassled. It's safer than the parks.'

'You've stayed there before?'

'For a few nights, yeah. There's parts undercover. Rotundas and the like.'

'Righto. Thanks.'

'Keep a low profile, though. If the staff spot you, you'll get turfed.'

He gives me directions.

'Thanks,' I say. 'And I hope it all works out.'

He frowns. 'What works out?'

'With the cancer.'

He shakes his head. 'How do you think it'll work out?'

I shrug. 'All the same.'

He nods. 'Yeah, all the same.'

Four

I walk up Russell Street, past a mix of Asian restaurants, then onto Lygon. Tourists crowd the footpath, spilling out of Italian cafes and chequer-clothed tourist traps. I pass a few restaurant spruikers, dressed in cheap dark suits and bright satin ties. None want my business.

The footpath is much busier than I remember. Every second person is on their mobile phone, talking loudly or typing on their screens. It's like I'm invisible. The parked cars look different too. Smoother and more metallic.

Near Elgin Street, I'm stopped by a skinny woman in an oversized Adidas jacket, her eyes glazed.

'Any change, brother?'

I search my pockets, give her the silver.

'Nothing else?'

'Sorry. I'm gonna need it.'

'Fair enough. God bless ya.'

Her gaze drifts to the next passer-by.

Could I beg on the street if things get desperate? Would I be up for it?

By the time I arrive at the main gate on College Crescent, it's late afternoon. The gates are tall and green, cast iron, with spikes at the top. To the left is the bluestone gatehouse, its Gothic arches bathed in soft afternoon light. I spot the sign for the office out back, a shiny red hatchback parked on the road beside. I decide to look for another way in.

Back on Lygon Street, I can see another gate maybe two hundred metres up ahead, opposite a tram stop. My feet are starting to hurt. My boots have dried and hardened in the years that've passed, locked away in a box somewhere. They feel smaller, almost like they might have belonged to someone else.

The gate on this side is more modern, in black steel and grey stone. A sign on the fence tells me the cemetery closes at 6 pm. There doesn't seem to be anyone around.

I go through the gate and up a neatly paved ramp with chrome handrails running its length. Black Italian graves with gold lettering line the entrance, a few adorned with lurid plastic flowers. Borsari, Modenesi, and Cuccinare. Their porcelain portraits watch me pass. A faded sign up ahead tells me that all dogs must be leashed.

A narrow road travels left and right, parallel to the Lygon Street fence. Two paths diverge up the hill, winding out of view. Aside from the Italian ones, the graves up ahead look very old and mostly in bad shape. Pretty unlikely to get visitors, I decide. I take the left-hand path up the hill.

Gum trees line the way, a few peppercorns, conifers too. Leaf and bark are strewn around the graves, dry weeds here and there. Some currawongs sing to one another from the trees, unseen. One calls, the other responds.

In the distance, through the trees, I see a large bluestone building at the crest of a hill. A mausoleum, maybe. I slow down, approach more carefully. There are two old women there, visiting a crypt on one side. Both are dressed in black, one is badly hunched over.

I crouch down and move off the main path, cross between graves, then down a narrower, broken concrete path, until the mausoleum is out of sight. The fewer people who see me here, the better.

This area seems even less travelled, the graves here more ancient, overgrown. Most are cracked and tilted askew by tree roots and time. Dry, twisted shrubs grow here and there. I pass the decaying sandstone grave of someone named Derrimut, a 'Native Chief' who died way back in 1864. Up ahead, to the left, I finally spot what I'm looking for.

The rotunda has a green iron roof and cream timber walls, its paint old and peeling. Inside, a timber bench circles the perimeter. If I'm lying down, I don't think I'll be visible. At least not by anyone walking the road. It can't be a popular spot for visitors, surely. A little further on, beside the road, I spot a garden tap.

I place my bag down on the bench, unzip it. I take out the thick, grey blanket I got from the Salvos. The lady didn't ask any questions, only smiled and wished me luck. I get a plastic bottle from my bag, go to the tap and fill it. I take a deep drink. It's cold and delicious. The beer is in my bag, but I'll save that for later.

In the distance, I can hear the traffic out on Lygon Street, the faint ding of a tram carried by the breeze. The sun is slowly getting lower in the sky, the air starting to cool. Maybe an hour til dusk.

I know it's not a long-term solution. Eventually, I'll be found and told to leave. More importantly, I'll run out of money before then.

Back in the rotunda, I sit on the bench. It feels good to be off my feet and away from people. If I squint my eyes, listen to the birds and the breeze through the trees, it's almost like I'm back in the country. I reach into my bag and take out the cheeseburger I bought along the way. I'm hungry, but I decide to wait. It'll give me something to look forward to.

I reach into my pocket and count the money. There's just $25.20 left.

Most likely it was that bastard behind the counter who stole my wallet, or maybe someone he told. Either way, there's little chance of getting it back.

I think again about the till at the bottle shop, the woman with hard eyes, then force the idea from my mind.

The currawongs start their call once more. I wonder what they're saying, whether they've noticed me. Time slowly draws out as the light begins to fade. I take off my boots, lay down on the bench, and close my eyes.

•

It's dark and cold when I wake. I'm not sure how much time has passed – maybe an hour or two. I sit up and pull the blanket around my shoulders.

The gates should be locked by now, so I should be safe from visitors. I reach into my bag, take out the cheeseburger and unwrap it. I eat as slowly as I can. It's soft and salty, the gherkin sweetly acidic, but it tastes good. I decide to drink the beer. It's warm and bitter, but I feel better for it. My head swims.

I get up and walk out of the rotunda. My eyes slowly adjust to the gloom, and I can make out the silhouettes of the graves around me. In the distance, I see the lights of the city. It's a good view from here. There seems to be more skyscrapers than

I remember, though I only saw the city skyline once or twice before.

I close my eyes and listen – the hum of traffic, a beeping horn, an ambulance siren carried by the wind. All of it seems far away. It feels safe here, secluded. Surely there's no-one else around.

I walk up the road, toward the light of the mausoleum. As I get closer, I slow down. I stop a little way short, sit on the edge of a large and decaying grave.

In Memory of John Alexander Burnett
Merchant
Who died 25 May 1853
Aged 36 years

Must've been someone important to get a grave this big. Either way, I figure he won't mind my company.

I unzip my jacket pocket, reach inside. I take out the envelope.

There's just enough light from the mausoleum to make out the words. But the truth is, I barely need to read it anymore. I know it almost off by heart.

Dear Tom,

I hope you're well. I'm so sorry I haven't been in touch, or taken your calls, but things have been really busy for me up here.

I've got a new job at a pub (that's three jobs now) and it's been a bit hectic. It's been good, though, because I'm saving some money for once, instead of just spending it. I'm hoping to get enough for a house deposit eventually. Nothing fancy, just a roof over my head. Like I've told you, Robert didn't leave me much when he died, apart from debts. And I don't want to be renting forever.

That's part of the reason I'm writing to you. And it's part of the reason I haven't been able to take your calls. To be honest, it's taken me a while to get the courage up to tell you.

A little while ago, I met someone. His name's Derek (yes, I know). He was a customer at the last pub I worked at, and we kinda hit it off. It wasn't something I was looking for, or expecting, but he's a very decent man. He's moving in with me soon, which will help with the rent and everything.

I know this will be painful for you to read. I wish things could have been different between us. I wish you hadn't gone to jail, that we could have had a chance. But it's just too hard now, and I'm too far away to make things work.

I'm sorry I didn't tell you sooner, but I hope you'll under-stand. And I really hope that you're doing okay. I know the time passes so slowly for you in there, but it won't be forever.

When you're out, we'll see each other again. And you'll always be welcome to visit me here. I know it's still a few years down the track, but still.

Again, I'm so sorry for not being in touch. Please know that I'll always be thinking of you.

X

L.

PS – I put your lucky charm in the envelope, so I hope they let you keep it. I think you might need it more than me.

I fold up the letter, push it back inside the envelope. I take a deep breath in and out. I reach inside my pocket, give the rabbit's foot a squeeze.

Once she moved back to Queensland, I knew it would be hard. Life would move on, things would change, while I'd stay the same. Being in prison was like being frozen in the past.

When she started refusing my calls, I wondered if I'd said something wrong. I can still remember our last conversation, replay it word for word. How she seemed so distant.

I can't blame her for moving on with her life. Nine years is a long time. Even so, there might be some faint hope. She said she'd like to see me, after all. Maybe I'll call her again sometime. Maybe she's still at the same place. I still know the number off by heart.

I decide to have a closer look at the mausoleum. It's built from bluestone, like the gatehouse, but it looks much newer. At this end are two large steel gates. Inside one is a room with a grey marble floor, beyond which is a wall of black granite, stacked with crypts. The light is dim, but I can see there are photos on most of them, bright plastic flowers here and there. Just inside the gate is a statue of the Virgin Mary, holding the baby Jesus.

I wonder why they need the gates, and why they're locked.

Must be to keep people out at night.

People like me.

To my left, just outside the mausoleum, is a tall stone pillar. It's maybe four metres high, with a bronze eagle at its top.

Pro Patria

Hungaria

1858

1956

I hear rustling in the grass. Rats, most likely. I decide to head back to the rotunda.

In the morning, I'll go to the Centrelink in Richmond. I'll try to get the one-off payment *The Big Issue* seller talked about. Maybe I can get a bus up to Brisbane, try to find her. It'd be good to see her, even if she's still with the new bloke. She did say she'd like to see me, after all.

Either way, it might be good to have a fresh start somewhere new. There's nothing and no-one keeping me here. Maybe I could do some fruit picking, some cash jobs here and there.

I lay down on the bench, kick off my boots, pull the blanket up to my chin. It feels good to have the beginnings of a plan.

And even though I'm sure the gates would be closed by now, I wonder if there might be others in here like me. Len can't be the only one who'd thought of it, after all.

I close my eyes and wait for sleep.

Five

‘Rise and shine, Sonny Jim.’

I open my eyes. There's a man standing over me, wearing green overalls. He's short and stocky. A wide smile, pale blue eyes.

‘You requested a wake-up call, right?’

I push my blanket aside, sit up. It's early, surely only just past dawn. My mouth is horribly dry.

‘You can't sleep here, mate, I'm sorry to say. The bosses don't like it. Couldn't give a fuck, myself. But I don't make the rules.’

He must be one of the cemetery staff, what Len warned me about.

I pull on my boots. A dog comes running into the rotunda, a blue staffy. It jumps up on my legs, tail wagging, bright eyes.

'Get down, Lina,' the man says. The dog ignores him.

'What time is it?'

'Just past seven. Our day begins when yours ends, as we like to say. It's kinda like our motto.'

'How'd you know I was here?'

'You got spotted on the security camera, up at the mausoleum. Motion sensors. We got them put in after some vandalism last year. Mostly picks up foxes or rats, but it's good for larger species too.'

He reaches into his pocket, takes out a soft pack of cigarettes. The dog goes to his side.

'You want one?'

I shake my head. 'I'll get moving.'

I roll up my blanket, push it into my bag.

'What's the rush?' He lights a cigarette. 'The name's Cyril.'

He holds out his hand. His skin is rough and dry, and he squeezes my fingers too tightly. I meet his gaze.

'Tom.'

'You got a surname?'

'Blackburn.'

'You don't look like a Blackburn.'

'Who do I look like?'

'Not a Blackburn.'

'You don't look like a Cyril, either.'

'Really? And what's a Cyril look like?'

I shrug.

He takes a deep drag of his cigarette, lets out a thick plume of smoke. He's not a big man, but he has the rugged solidity of manual labour. His skin is dark and weathered from too much sun, his nose thick and crooked, maybe broken once or twice. He sits down on the bench opposite me, a smile at the edge of his lips.

'So, what brought you to this here Eden?'

I watch the smoke drift from the end of his cigarette. 'I got told it was a good place to crash. That it's safe. Guess that was wrong.'

'Oh, it's safe alright. Like I said, it's mostly just foxes and rats around at night. Occasionally we get some schoolkids on a dare, which is why we've got the cameras.' He takes another drag of his cigarette. 'You been on the streets a while?'

'Nah.'

'Didn't think so. What happened then?'

'What do you mean?'

'Well, you don't look like you're on the gear. You got a screw loose?'

'Is that a prerequisite?'

He whistles. 'Jeez, a bit touchy. Not a morning person, I gather. Were you inside then?'

The dog gets up and comes over to my feet. She lets out a sigh, then lays down.

'Listen,' he says, 'I've been around a while. I've made pretty much every mistake under the sun, so there's no judgement here.'

I lean down and zip up my bag. 'I better get moving.'

'Christ, have I offended you? I don't get much practice chatting with the permanent residents, to be fair. They're not very talkative, if you catch my drift.' He stands up. 'Listen, why don't you come back to the shed. I'll make you a coffee, then you can hit the road.'

I'd kill for a coffee, but I wonder what he wants. I look him in the eye, try to get a read.

'I promise I won't bite. Look, I know how shit rolls your way sometimes, no matter what you do. You think this was part of my grand plan? To work in a cemetery?'

I shrug.

'Well, it wasn't. But I fucking love it now. This is like my own private paradise, you know? All one hundred and six acres. And the people here are like family, even the ones in the ground. It's as close as you can get to God, I'd say, if I believed in the bastard. And it's right in the middle of the city. I'm not religious at all, but this is a sacred place. I've witnessed some glorious things, things you wouldn't believe.'

He takes a last drag of his cigarette, flicks it out of the rotunda.

'C'mon, I'll get you that coffee. Then you can be on your way.'

•

Cyril leads the way from the rotunda, along a winding road through the middle of the cemetery. Lina follows, ducking between the graves, pissing here and there.

'She doesn't mean any offence,' he says. 'She can smell the foxes. Just marking her territory.'

Up ahead, at the end of the road, there's a set of iron gates. Just before the exit, on the right, is a large steel shed with a roller door. A white Toyota Hilux ute with the cemetery logo is parked on a grassy verge nearby.

'This is all pretty new,' he says. 'The shed, I mean. It used to be way over the other side, near Princes Park, but there's another mausoleum there now. There's fuck-all room for new graves, so they're stacking them up to bring in some revenue. The Italians love it, of course. They're all dying to get in here, you know.'

'Funny.'

He shakes his head. 'Tough crowd.'

He opens a door beside the roller door.

'After you,' he says.

It's dark inside the shed, and at least a few degrees cooler. Near the roller door is a bright yellow mechanical digger. Beside that is a four-wheeler, with some mowing equipment behind. Against the wall there's an assortment of garden tools: shovels, spades, and pickaxes. Cyril steps past me and gestures toward a timber bench on one side.

'Take a seat. How do you like your coffee?'

'White, two sugars.'

'Gotcha.'

I hear a toilet flush, then a door opens to my right. A tall man with a long goatee steps out, holding a newspaper.

'Who the fuck is this?' he says.

'Seamus, this is Tom. Tom this is Seamus. Seamus is Irish. He's also a prick.'

Lina runs to Seamus and jumps at his legs. He pushes her away.

'What's he doing here?' he says to Cyril.

'Security spotted him on the cameras last night, so they put in a call to the office. I found him sleeping in one of the rotundas. You know I got a sixth sense when there's someone around, I can always track them down.'

Cyril goes through a doorway against the back wall. I hear a tap running, the filling of a kettle. Seamus walks past me, leans down, and opens the roller door. The morning light floods inside.

Cyril calls from out back. 'You gonna make a start on that grave, Seamus?'

'Yeah, I'll get the measurements done. I'll see you out there.'

He climbs aboard the four-wheeler, starts it up and drives out. After a few minutes, Cyril returns with two mugs, passes one to me.

'Thanks.'

'No worries.' He sits his mug down on the bench. 'I'll grab us some biscuits.'

I sip my coffee. It's hot and sweet. Lina climbs into a fleecy bed near the back of the shed and eyes me sleepily. Cyril returns with half a packet of Arnott's Assorted.

'Here,' he says. 'Reckon you're probably starving.'

I grab a few at once. 'Coffee's good.'

He sits down on the bench, stretches his legs out. 'Just instant, but it'll do in a pinch.' He blows on his coffee, takes a sip. 'So, what's your plan from here? You got somewhere to stay?'

I eat a cream-filled biscuit. It's stale and much too sweet, but I'm happy for it all the same.

'Probably gonna head up to Queensland.'

'You got a car?'

'I'll get the bus or something.'

'You've got family up there?'

'Nah.'

'Anyone here?'

'Nah. My parents are dead.'

'No brothers or sisters?'

I shake my head.

'Why Queensland then?'

'I know someone up there.'

'Let me guess. It's a woman, right?'

I shrug.

'She know you're coming?'

'Nah.'

'Jeez, mate. It's a long way to go for a surprise visit. How much cash you got?'

'Not much.'

'Enough for the bus?'

'Probably not.'

'How you gonna manage it then?'

'What's it to you?'

'Just curious.'

'I was gonna try Centrelink.'

He nods. 'Fair enough. Maybe you should get in touch with her first, though.'

I look over at Lina, fast asleep in her bed. 'What do you care?'

'Look, it's none of my business, but you could end up in the same situation. And I'm not sure the cemeteries in Queensland are quite as hospitable.'

I take another sip of my coffee.

'What did you used to do?' he says. 'Before you went inside, I mean?'

'Bit of this, bit of that.'

'Any good on the tools?'

'Depends.'

'And who's this woman you wanna see?'

'Just someone.'

'An old flame?'

'Maybe.'

'Fuck, mate, it's like getting blood from a stone with you.'

I shrug.

'Listen, I just had a thought. We just lost one of our men here, a few weeks back. One of our cemetery technicians.'

'Technicians?'

'Just a fancy name for a gravedigger. He decided he'd had enough, so it's just me and that Irish prick at the moment. And if he's off sick, I'm on my own, which makes it just about imposs-ible. We're gonna hire someone soon enough, but we'll have to advertise and all that. Bit of a process. I could use an extra set of hands in the meantime. Just a drudge, nothing glamorous. Honest, physical work. Bit of gardening, bit of digging, bit of whatever the fuck I tell you. Some days will be shitful, but it'll get you some experience. And some cash.'

'I'll get paid?'

'Sure. But first I need to know that you're not a nutter. That you're not gonna hear some voices and decide to stick a knife in me. Or a kiddie fiddler. I couldn't abide that.'

'If I was, would I tell you?'

He nods. 'Fair enough. But I have to ask, all the same. Let's just call it a bit of due diligence.'

'I'm neither.'

'What did you do, then? To end up inside?'

I take another biscuit out of the packet. A Scotch finger. It's buttery and delicious. I look out the roller door as the sun slowly rises above a line of tall pine trees. I can hear a honeyeater calling, a car driving past on the road outside. I drink the last of my coffee, want another.

'You really need to know?'

'Can't let you stay unless you tell me.'

I swallow. My mouth dry. 'Accessory to murder.'

'No shit?'

'No shit.'

'What happened?'

'Helped out a mate who was in a spot. It got me nine years.'

'You regret it?'

I lean forward, put the empty mug at my feet.

'I regret some things, but I did what I thought was right at the time. I owed him.'

'And now?'

I shrug. 'I'd probably do the same, if I had my time again.'

'So, you helped him dump the body?'

'Something like that.'

'Well, that pretty much counts as a qualification round here.' He grins. 'Let's call it recognition of prior learning.'

I shake my head. 'It's been a long time. Since I've had a job, I mean.'

'Look, we can just see how we go, take it day by day. No commitment either way. And I'll pay you cash in hand, in case you need to go to Centrelink after. Keep you off the books.

Plus, you can sleep here in the shed, as long as you keep it clean. There's a shower out back, a little kitchen.'

I look around. It's definitely a step up from the rotunda. And the cash would be more than helpful.

'What's the catch?'

He leans forward.

'Mate, there is no catch. I just need the extra set of hands, and you look like you could use a break. Everyone deserves a second chance in my book. Plus, I get a good feeling about you. My instincts are rarely off the mark. But, like I said, it won't be long term. Just until we hire someone. Someone with actual qualifications, you know? That's what the boss wants, at least. Horticultural or the like, not the kind you get from the old Bluestone College. Most of the work around here is gardening. We usually get contractors in for the mowing, but money's a bit tight at the moment. Bottom line is that I can't pay you much. Still, it'll be better than nothing.'

I nod. 'Fair enough.'

'So, we got a deal then?'

I get the feeling I'm not being told something, but I'm not sure what.

He holds out his hand, I give it a squeeze.

'Yep, deal.'

Part Two

One

'You sure this is a good idea?' Seamus glares at me, then Cyril. 'Could get us properly in the shit, you know.'

Cyril shakes his head. 'You leave that to me.'

'Krystal's not gonna like it.'

He lights a cigarette. 'I'll have a chat to her and sort it. She knows we're in a bit of a spot at the moment. We can't afford to fall any further behind.'

Cyril takes a crinkled map from his shirt pocket, unfolds it. He traces his finger down the centre, then to the left. Lina sits at his feet.

'This is definitely it,' he says. 'But it always pays to double-check. Isn't that right, Seamus?'

Seamus leans on his spade. 'Never let me forget that one, will you?'

Cyril grins and turns to me. 'We got a metre or so down and found an existing tenant who wasn't too pleased about the disturbance. Hell of a pain in the arse. You've gotta notify the police, who then get the coroner involved. Can take forever. Even when we do check we've got the right gravesite, we still come across a body sometimes. Some of the old graves were unmarked because the families couldn't afford a headstone. A pauper's grave, you might say. Record keeping wasn't too flash back in the day, so we come across them every now and again.'

He folds the map and pushes it into his pocket.

'Anyway, this one is definitely vacant. According to the map, at least.'

It looks a narrow plot, sandwiched between two existing graves. On the right is someone named Patrick Mahoney, a magistrate who died in 1912, and his wife, Margaret, who followed two years later. To the left is a family of four, the Callaghans, the last of whom departed in 1892. Both graves are badly askew. The magistrate's headstone, made of granite, looks on the brink of collapse.

'They didn't do foundations the same way back then,' Cyril says. 'Usually just some bricks on the ground. The mortar wasn't as good, either. Not much cement in it, mostly just sand. So a lot of them collapse after a while, especially if there's some tree roots nearby. We can't afford to fix them, of course. Unless there are some wealthy descendants who pay to get a stonemason in. Pretty rare, though.'

He butts out his cigarette, flicks it between the two graves opposite.

'On the plus side, they had some beautiful stone back in the old days. Scottish granite, marble from Italy. They used to ship it over from Europe as ballast. There're some iron headstones too, from the Industrial Revolution, but those are pretty rare. They even used to do them in timber sometimes, way back when. But they stopped because people used to steal them for firewood.'

'No shit?' I say.

He hocks something in his throat, spits it out. 'Desperate times and desperate people, you know. These days, most of the stone comes from China. The local stonemasons are a dying breed. A lot of them are just glorified salesmen, doing their level best to guilt the grieving into some elaborate monument they can't afford.'

He plants his spade into the earth.

'Anyway, enough of the history lesson. Let's get to the practical. There's more to this than you might think, so watch and learn.'

He takes out a measuring tape.

'It's a standard measurement, but it always pays to double-check. Belts and braces, you know. Occasionally the standard doesn't fit, because some of the graves here were done pretty rough. When that happens, we have to improvise, but this one looks okay. We go twenty-one hundred long, about six-fifty wide, give or take. Sometimes, the occupied graves encroach from the side, but you won't know that until you start digging. I guess they like to check out who their new neighbour is.'

He marks out the measurement with four wooden pegs.

'Occasionally, we'll get some fat bastard who doesn't fit a standard grave. Those ones have to buy two graves, side by side. Sometimes we even have to get a crane in for the burial, because no-one can lift the fucker. Quite the scene. Anyway, we'll dig this down a little way, just so we've got the right shape for the Wacker.'

'The Wacker?'

'The Wacker Neuson.' He points toward the mechanical digger up on the footpath. 'That's his proper name, but he prefers Wacker for short. He's German, so don't mention the war and all that.'

Seamus takes his spade and quickly digs out a shallow rectangle, careful to work along the edge as marked. Cyril starts up the digger. It splutters a few times, then rumbles to life. He shouts above the noise.

'When I started, we had to do a fair chunk of this grunt work by hand. It nearly broke you. Bloody dangerous too, because you don't want to be down in there if she collapses. These days no-one's allowed in the grave, so we do as much as we can with the machine. The blade on it is made especially for this kinda work. Sometimes there's isn't much room, and it can be hard to get the Wacker in. But we make it fit, even if it means making some adjustments to the nearby graves. Taking off their headstones and such, assuming they're not too fragile. But we try to avoid doing that if we can.'

He brings the digger forward and into position and starts excavating, methodically depositing an increasing mound of clay nearby.

Seamus leans on his spade, gestures toward the deepening grave.

'Sometimes it can be a bit unstable,' he says. 'Only a few parts of the cemetery are like that, mostly on the Princes Park side. We're lucky it's mostly clay in this place, a bit of rock here and there. In some of the other cemeteries, you can't get very far without it collapsing, especially if it's been raining a bit. Out at Fawkner, they have to dig them on the day of the burial. Any further out and they'll collapse. Pain the arse. It's not as bad here, but we always keep an eye out for cracks, just in case. More often you'll get the tree roots. There are some big fucken trees in this place, in case you haven't noticed, and some big fucken roots. They can be a nightmare to get through. Tough as hell.'

Cyril slowly digs deeper and deeper. Seamus stands beside the grave, giving directions about where he needs to go wider.

'Once he's done,' Seamus says, 'we'll neaten the edges with the spades. Has to look good for the family, you know. The sort of thing they tend to notice.'

'Who's being buried?'

He picks up a spade. 'Some old bloke. Burial's tomorrow, which is a bit tight. Normally we dig it at least two days out, but we're well behind at the moment.'

'How deep do you go?'

'Twenty-two hundred for this one, because it's a double. Seventeen hundred if it's a single. Occasionally you get a triple, but that's pretty rare. We go a bit deeper than we used to, because the coffins are bigger. Partly because people are fatter than they used to be, but mostly because the undertakers upsell the big, expensive coffins.'

I think of my mum and wonder if she got a good one for her burial, or if it was something cheap. I push the thought away.

'Once we're done with the excavation,' Seamus says, 'we cover the grave with a sheet of plywood. Just so no silly bugger falls in before the burial. In this case, his wife will be joining him later. Often happens pretty quick, you know. Especially if they've been married a long time. It's like they've always been a double act, and the one left behind can't cope going solo. You'll see them here visiting the grave, day after day, get to know them too. Next thing, you're burying them.'

The mountain of clay is getting bigger, seemingly bigger than the hole itself. Seamus sees me looking.

'Bit of an eyesore, I know, but not much we can do about it. We'll cover it up with some rolls of fake turf once we're done. It's pretty confronting for the family to see all that and know it's going to be piled on top of their loved one. But it looks just as bad once it's filled in. Takes an age for it to settle, but you need to let nature take its course. If you tamp it down, it can break the coffin.'

'Has that happened?'

He shakes his head. 'You only ever make mistakes like that once. But we try to keep it all as neat as we can, you know. There's a bit of an art to this business, a bit of theatre. It's not something you can just pick up overnight, despite what Cyril might tell you. But you'll get the hang of it.'

I look up as a middle-aged man walks past on the footpath, leading a large German shepherd. He glances at the grave, looks away. Lina stands and watches them pass.

'We get a few dog walkers in here,' Seamus says. 'Usually the antisocial ones that can't cope with the park. The dogs, I mean. The owners too, probably. We used to get a few stray cats, but Lina took care of them. Cyril can't stand them.'

'Hate the fuckers,' he yells out. 'Kill the native wildlife, you know? The number of dead little ringtails I find, some beautiful birds too. They're the worst kind of vermin in my book. I'd take the foxes any day.'

Once Cyril gets deep enough, he pulls the Wacker back and cuts the engine.

'Righto, Tom. Your turn now. But I'll leave you with Seamus. I've got to drop into the office for a quick chat with the powers that be.'

Seamus passes me a spade.

'This bit isn't rocket science,' he says. 'The Wacker's blade does a pretty good job, as you can see, but we just want to make sure it's as plumb and square as possible all the way down. Aside from the aesthetics, it means the coffin can get lowered smoothly and without any hitches.'

'Hitches?'

'Like if it gets stuck. Happened just the once since I've been here. A bit like breaking a coffin, it's the sort of mistake you'll only ever make once. Caused a hell of a scene.'

'What happened?'

He scratches at his goatee. 'Well, we usually keep a low profile for the burial, unless the undertaker needs help lowering the coffin. Mourners usually don't like to see us around, you know. But for this one, Kev was on hand. He worked here until recently. Anyway, the coffin got stuck about halfway, which is about as bad as it gets.'

He starts cutting the edges with his spade.

'What he should've done was lift the coffin back out, then widen the sides where she was catching. It would have been an ugly scene, but still. Instead, he took a short cut which was a hundred times worse. He got inside the grave, on top of the coffin, and stomped it down.'

'Christ.'

He nods. 'Needless to say, the family weren't too impressed. He was lucky to keep his job. Cyril took some of the heat and saved his skin.'

'But he left anyway?'

'Yeah, he met some girl who didn't like this line of work. Emily, her name was.'

Seamus leans his spade against an adjacent headstone.

'Listen, you sure you're up for all this?'

I dust some dirt off my jeans. 'I reckon so.'

He scratches his cheek. 'There's a bit more to the job than meets the eye, you know.'

I get the feeling he wants to tell me something, but isn't sure how to say it.

'I'll be right.'

He narrows his eyes. 'Let me put it this way. If I were you and I had another option, I'd take it. Once you start here, it can be pretty hard to leave.'

'Kev did, though.'

He sighs. 'Yeah, true enough.' He picks up his spade. 'C'mon, let's get this done. Burial's tomorrow, remember. And we've still got another one to do.'

I watch as Seamus cuts at the edges of the grave. I try to do the same on the other side. He's definitely holding something back.

'How long you been here?' I say.

'Five years. Did bar work when I first got here, at one of those godawful Irish-themed pubs. That's where I met Cyril. He was one of the customers.'

'What'd you do back in Ireland?'

'Used to be a painter. Family business. My dad had the contracts to paint the lighthouses on the islands. I was never much chop at school, so I left early and started working with him. A good job, as long as you enjoy your own company and don't mind the wet and the cold.'

'Why'd you leave?'

He chips out a stone from the edge. 'Economy tanked, you know. Irish Tiger and all that. The banks loaned too much and fucked pretty much everyone sideways. Dad's business was still doing okay, paying the bills. But I met this girl, Rachel, and she was coming here to look for work. So, I came with her.'

'You're still together?'

His face clouds over.

'She's dead.'

'Shit. Sorry.'

'Yeah, me too.'

'What happened?'

He shakes his head. 'Tell you some other time. C'mon, let's get this done before that fucker and his dog get back. Won't hear the end of it, otherwise.'

·

The second grave proves more difficult. There's a thick and gnarly tree root from a nearby oak, and we're forced to cut through it with an extendable saw. Cyril sits in the Wacker, watching our progress, barking orders every now and again.

'Once you get through that bastard, I'll do the rest.'

It's been a long time since I've done manual labour, any labour really, and my hands soon blister. I wish I had some gloves, but I don't want to ask. I grit my teeth and try to push through it.

'Good stuff,' Cyril says. He starts up the Wacker. 'I'll get the rest done, then you boys tidy up. After that, I reckon it's time for a beer.'

•

Once the second grave's ready, we head back to the shed. Cyril drives the Wacker with Lina in his lap, while I follow on foot. Seamus drives the four-wheeler slowly beside me. On the way, we pass a young woman tending a gravesite. She glances at me, then looks away.

'Better get used to that,' Seamus says. 'A mixed bag with the visitors. Some want to chat, others look at you like you're the Grim Reaper. I think she falls into the latter category. But we try to say hello to most of the people. You'd be surprised, but there's a bit of community here. We get to know the regulars. Some have been coming every day for years. Rain, hail, or shine.'

There's a twisting feeling in my stomach. My mum's grave, I've never even seen it.

'Every day?' I say.

He nods. 'But even if they're up for a chat, grief is mostly a private thing. It's between them and whoever's in the grave.

Some people sing songs, have long conversations, talk about the weather, all sorts of shit. Sometimes, they even have little parties on the dead person's birthday, with booze and music. Whatever gets you through, you know.'

Once we arrive at the shed, Cyril gets three cans from the fridge.

'Not for me,' Seamus says. 'Gotta get moving.'

Cyril frowns. 'At least stick around for the welcoming ceremony. Only take a minute.'

He goes out back, returns with a filthy hi-vis jacket. 'Nearest thing we've got to a uniform.' He throws it to me.

'Thanks.'

'So, I guess that means you're hired. For now, at least.' Cyril cracks his can, raises it, takes a deep drink. 'But listen, if Krystal from the office asks you, you gotta say we're old mates, right? We go way back.'

I crack my can, take a sip. It's cold and bitter.

Seamus picks up his bike from against the shed wall. 'Catch you both tomorrow.' He looks at me. 'Don't let this bloke chew your ear off. A couple of beers and he starts thinking he's Aristotle. Do your head in.'

He goes out through the roller door.

Cyril calls out after him. 'Just make sure you're here early. Two burials tomorrow, remember?'

I sit down on the bench. My legs ache, my hands throb. I feel as hungry as I've been in years. Cyril sits across from me in the Wacker. He kicks off his boots, lights a cigarette. Lina watches us from her bed.

'So, how'd you find it?'

'Hard.'

He smiles, takes a drag. 'It'll get easier. But no two days are ever the same. It's part of what I love about the place.'

I take a deeper drink. Cyril eyes me.

'So, did your mate ever thank you?'

'Which mate?'

'The one you helped. With the body.'

I twist at the ring-pull, break it off.

'Not really.'

'You still in touch?'

'Nah.'

'How come?'

'He's dead.'

'What happened?'

I let him down, that's what happened.

'He killed himself.'

Cyril shakes his head. 'We get a few like that here. They're the worst, I gotta say. Especially if they're kids. For the family, I mean. I guess they think they're doing the right thing, but it ruins the lives of those around them.'

He butts out his cigarette against the Wacker.

'I spose they think life's too painful, or not worth living. Or their loved ones might be better off without them. I know some people say it's selfish, but I don't think like that. Life can be pretty fucking meaningless at times. We try to give it meaning, trick ourselves into thinking there's some kinda purpose that makes it worthwhile. But the truth is, there's no real sense to life.'

I start to feel very tired.

'Camus talks about this stuff. He said there's no meaning of life, or words to that effect. Or maybe it was Sartre. Always get those two mixed up.'

'Is this what Seamus warned me about?'

He lets out a burp. 'Just stuff I read about, unlike him. Philosophy interests me, I guess. But he's mostly into reading the form guide.'

'A gambler?'

He lights another cigarette. 'You could say that. You could also say he's an idiot. But he's a mate, and I'm loyal to my mates. Look, I'm no expert on the philosophical stuff, but I've learnt a bit. I don't have a telly at home, so I mostly read. Just because I dig graves for a living doesn't mean I have to be ignorant. And working in a place like this makes you question the big picture, especially when you're burying kids. No sense in that.'

He takes a deep drag, lets out a plume of blue smoke.

'Did you go to his funeral?'

'Whose?'

'Your mate.'

I shake my head. 'I was inside.'

The day I got the news, that copper with cold eyes. The hollow feeling that never left.

'Ah, that's a shame. An important ceremony, you know? Some people don't really get it. But once you go through it, you understand. We humans need that sort of stuff. We're social creatures, and it helps mark what we're all going through. It's one of the few things that separates us from animals. But even animals have their rituals, right?'

A heavier fatigue begins to wash over me. I want to lie down and close my eyes. I want Cyril to stop talking.

'Why did he kill him? I'm guessing it was a bloke he knocked off. He didn't kill his wife or girlfriend, did he?'

The darkness in the clearing, the empty look in his eyes.

'I'd rather not talk about it.'

He nods. 'Fair enough. I get the feeling I need to tread lightly with you. Another beer?'

'I'm pretty knackered.'

'Just one more. You grab it.'

In the fridge out back, I see a pack of sliced ham and half a loaf of bread. My stomach rumbles. I bring back two beers.

'By the way, there's a couple of cans of baked beans in the cupboard for later. Microwave out there too.'

'Thanks.'

'What goes around comes around, you know? Life can deal you some pretty shitful cards. A lot of people like to think the world's a level playing field, but that's bullshit.'

I crack my can.

'How'd you end up working here?'

He sighs, takes a deep drink.

'A long story, but I'll save it for another day. Bottom line is that I didn't have much choice.'

'You mean you were forced?'

He shakes his head. 'Not exactly. The way I see it, we have no real control over our lives, no matter what we think. We're just biological machines, like any other animal. We didn't choose the brains we got, the childhood we had. Even so, we like to think we're in charge, that we have a choice.'

'You think we don't have any choice? Over anything?'

He nods. 'Bit of a headfuck, I know. Let me put it another way. Pretty much the only thing that exists in the universe is cause and effect, right? Like, if I push you now, you'll fall off that bench. Physicists have known about that forever. So this idea that there's some mystical power called "free will" is just horseshit. It's like believing in the supernatural, or religion. It's that far-fetched.'

He takes a drag of his cigarette. 'You think you decided to come here to the cemetery?'

I nod. 'I could've gone anywhere.'

'But you didn't. You came here. You didn't realise it, but all the moments in your life, and moments before your life, led to that decision. It was the only choice you could've made. Think about it. If free will existed, people would be going around doing all sorts of random shit. Instead, we all do mostly what's expected.'

I look out through the roller door as a cyclist passes. 'But if what you're saying's right, that we've got no real choice, then what's the point of doing anything?'

'Well, even if we don't have a choice, it's probably not a bad thing if we think that we do. And just because the future is pre-determined, it doesn't mean it's predictable. Chaos theory, you know?'

'I don't.'

He butts out his cigarette.

'We don't know what's coming, so it's worth sticking around to find out. Your life is kinda like a movie that's already been made. You don't know how it's gonna end, or if there's gonna be some twist, so it's worth waiting until it finishes. Unless the movie is intolerably bad, which I guess is how it was for your mate.'

He drinks the last of his can, hops off the Wacker.

'Anyway, I get the feeling you've heard enough from me. You look like you're about to drop dead. Luckily, you're in the right place.'

I roll my eyes.

He grins. 'I'll leave you to enjoy your evening. There's a radio in the kitchen if you get lonely, but try not to disturb the neighbours. They're heavy sleepers, but still.'

Two

The next morning, I wake before dawn. There's a tight, throbbing pain between my shoulder blades. Somehow, the bench here is even more uncomfortable than the one in the rotunda.

It makes me think of my last cellmate, Danny, who complained about his mattress more than anything else. He was just nineteen, his first stint in adult prison. Drug-related offending, some burgs, then an armed robbery gone badly wrong. Him and his mate tried to rob a convenience store in Sunshine, but the attendant resisted. Danny hit him just once in the side of the head with a baseball bat, and that was enough. A split-second decision ended one man's life, ruined another's.

He wasn't a bad kid, just a bit messed up. I wonder how he's doing in there.

I go out back to the kitchen, flick on the light. I make myself a coffee, then take the remaining half-can of baked beans from the fridge. I take both to the bench, eat the baked beans cold. I think about having a shower. Maybe later.

I wonder who came looking for me back at the hostel. The man with the limp. There couldn't be many people who knew I was getting out, probably no-one. Unless someone kept track over the years. Maybe that copper who questioned me way back when, but why would he?

It has to be Ali.

The time he served in Acacia Unit would've been brutal. Twenty-two hours a day in solitary, then two hours recreation with the prison's most dangerous. For someone with his particular brand of paranoia, it would've been a misery.

Before he got pinched for the drugs, he'd told me about the manslaughter that got him slotted. Tortured a bloke he reckoned had lagged to the coppers. Pliers and a bolt cutter.

'Squealed like a stuck pig.'

A chill runs through me.

Maybe it was bullshit that someone was looking for me. Maybe the guy behind the counter was just fucking with me.

Either way, I should be safe. Even if Ali knew I was at the hostel, he couldn't know I'm here.

When the time came, I hadn't bothered applying for parole. Some blokes played the game, said the right things, just to get out early. I didn't blame them. But I had nowhere to go and there was no-one waiting for me.

Ever since I'd gotten the letter, I'd pretty much resigned myself to life inside. In some ways, it was probably a blessing. The feeling that I was missing out on life with her slowly receded. Instead, my world compressed to what was inside those walls. For better or worse, it forced me to accept it.

Maybe that's why she did it. An act of mercy. Maybe it isn't true that she met someone else.

I try not to think about what happened, what got me put inside. It was so long ago, almost twenty years, and other prisoners had mostly stopped asking. It got a bit of press when I was sentenced, so when I first went inside most of them already knew.

As it turned out, it worked in my favour. They all saw me as a bit of a hero, even if the judge didn't see it that way.

During the first year, I often lay in bed at night replaying events, thinking I could have done things differently. But I learned there was no point going down that road. It made the time more of a struggle, and it was bad enough as it was.

The main problem was managing the fear, with a lot of unstable people in a confined space. Some, like Ali, were mad or bad or both. There'd be regular bursts of violence, a few murders. But one screw gave me some advice on my very first day. He told me to keep my head down, but not to show weakness either.

'It's a chook pen in here,' he said. 'And the weak get pecked to death.'

I finish my beans, put the can on the bench. I lift the roller door open and fresh air rushes inside, cool and crisp. I breathe in deeply. It's just before first light, and the gates will still be locked.

Truth is, I don't regret what I did. I just regret getting caught. More than that, I wish I could've done something to help my mate when it mattered, before it all got so out of control. The times I sensed something was wrong, but did nothing.

I decide to take a walk.

•

Cyril is waiting inside when I get back to the shed. He's sitting on the bench.

'Thought you might've shot through,' he says. 'By the way, is it your birthday today?'

I shake my head.

'Well, I got you a present anyway.' He throws me a black garbage bag. 'Some new clothes.'

'Really?'

He gets out his cigarettes, lights one. He takes a deep drag.

'Don't get too excited. I stopped at the op shop on the way home last night, so I can't promise it's high fashion. Actually, I can pretty much guarantee it's not. Probably some dead bloke's, but it was the best I could do in a pinch.'

'Thanks.'

'I also brought my inflatable mattress, but you'll have to blow it up yourself. Lost the pump years ago. You had breakfast?'

I nod.

'Well, I'll get you some more grub later. Nothing fancy, though.'

Over a coffee, Cyril tells me the plan for the day's work. Most of it revolves around the burials, but he doesn't want me to hang around for them.

'Just keep a low profile when the families arrive. No offence, but you don't look too flash. And you might look even worse in those clothes. You can help out once they've left, though. Just wait until the last car goes out through the gate. Any sign of Seamus yet?'

I shake my head.

'The slack fuck. You can see why I need an extra man. Especially since Kev up and left with sweet little Eleanor.'

'Yeah, Seamus told me. Emily, wasn't it?'

'Nah, definitely Eleanor. Real saintly type.' He shrugs. 'To be fair, I'd sensed something amiss so I started riding him pretty hard. I reckon he probably just wasn't up for it anymore. Happens from time to time. It takes a bit of steel to do this kinda work, you know. It isn't the most complex job, I'll give you that, but you need to be reliable.'

I nod. 'Fair enough. No Lina today?'

He smiles. 'Jesus, I love that little dog. But she gets a bit excited around strangers. Not everyone loves dogs, you know. Hard to believe, but true. And when people are mourning, emotions can run pretty high.'

'How long you had her?'

'Five years. Named her after someone I used to know. Someone pretty special to me.'

'An old flame?'

He flicks his cigarette butt out through the roller door. There's a smile at the edge of his lips.

'Not exactly. Listen, why don't you go get changed. I want you to drop something off at the office for me. It'll be a good chance for you to say g'day to Krystal, keep things above board.'

I go out back and open the garbage bag. Inside are three pairs of jeans, some t-shirts, a couple of woollen jumpers, a zip-up jacket, and some new underwear and socks, still in their plastic packets. I strip down, try on a pair of black jeans. They're a little loose on the waist, so I loop through my belt. I put on a yellow t-shirt, 'Ricardo's Plumbing Supplies', then a plain grey woollen jumper over the top. The wool is scratchy on my arms, but it feels better to be in some clean clothes.

When I come back out, Cyril is arranging tools against the wall.

'Christ, get a look at you. Like a rat with a gold tooth. Oh, nearly forgot. Here's a little something for your first day.' He takes out his wallet, passes me a twenty. 'Just something to whet your appetite. I'll fix you up for the rest later in the week.'

'Thanks.'

He reaches into his back pocket, takes out an envelope.

'Go over to the office and give this to Krystal for me. And don't forget how me and you go way back, right?'

'What should I tell her?'

'I said we worked together on a farm out west, but that's all she knows. You can fill in the blanks.'

A farm out west.

Cyril must know more than he let on. Maybe he read about me in the papers when I was sentenced. Maybe he's trying to test me.

He looks at me and frowns. 'Is there something else?'

'Nah, all good. I'll see you in a bit.'

On my way out of the shed, Seamus rides his bike in through the gate. I wait as he dismounts.

'Still here, then?' he says.

'Yep.'

'How'd you sleep?'

'Shithouse.'

He grins. 'Can't imagine that bench is too comfy. Where you off to now?'

'Dropping something off to Krystal. The office is over on the other side, right?'

He frowns. 'Did Cyril ask you?'

'Yep.'

He takes off his helmet, cuts his eyes at me.

'Already got you doing his dirty work.'

'Dirty work?'

He shakes his head. 'Never mind. Say hello to Krystal for me.'

•

I walk quickly along the road, North Avenue, through the centre of the cemetery. Signs point me toward the office. Along the way, I spot another mausoleum, a much newer looking one made of sharp angles and grey stone, nearer the Princes Park side. I wonder how they prepare for those funerals. I can't imagine there's much to it.

When I get closer to the office, I spot the same red hatchback outside. It's a shiny Volkswagen Golf. There's a bright pink sticker in the corner of the rear window.

> *Good girls go to heaven,*
> *Bad girls go everywhere.*

I run my fingers through my hair, straighten my jumper. As I open the door, I hear a phone ringing. The room has high ceilings, dark timber panelled walls, and a long wooden counter runs across its width. Leadlight windows let in the morning light. It feels old world, almost like a church.

There's movement out back, and a woman comes in through a doorway. She's maybe in her mid-thirties, with dyed blonde hair pulled back into a ponytail. Deep red lipstick. She wears a crisply ironed white shirt with a navy-blue cemetery logo on one side of her chest. A gold chain dangles inside her shirt.

'You must be the new boy.'

'Yeah, I'm Tom.'

'Krystal.'

'Unusual name.'

'My mum was into *Dynasty*, and she didn't have much imagination. Cyril sent you?'

I nod.

'So, I guess you've got something for me?'

She taps her fingernails on the counter. They're extremely long, painted bright pink. A large diamond sparkles on her ring finger.

I reach into my back pocket, hand her the envelope. She slides it into a drawer behind the counter, then locks it. She looks me up and down.

'Nice threads.'

'Fashion doesn't really interest me.'

'No kidding. So, how you settling in? The boys showing you the ropes?'

'Yeah. All good so far.'

She nods. 'Cyril's been around forever. Just do what he says and you'll be right. It's good to have an extra man on board. We've been a bit short-staffed since Kev left.'

'I heard.'

She frowns. 'Cyril says you two go way back, but you look a bit younger than I expected. A different vintage to him, at least.'

I feel my face getting hot.

'Clean living.'

She smiles, bright white teeth. 'That doesn't sound like much fun. So, how did you two meet?'

'We worked on a farm together.'

'He said as much. What kind of farm?'

'Sheep.'

'Were you a shearer?'

'Bit of this, bit of that.'

'Jack of all trades, master of none?'

I swallow. 'Something like that.'

'Not much of a talker, are you?'

'Guess not.'

'Not such a bad thing in my book. Some people bang on forever, and it drives me crazy. Take Cyril, for example. That bloke can talk underwater. You're not into philosophy too, are you?'

'Nah.'

'Thank God for that. He's about as much as I can take. He loves to get metaphysical. I think working in this place has done it to him. I guess it does make you question things, when you're faced with death so often. Makes you appreciate the good stuff too, because you know it won't last forever.'

'I thought you weren't into philosophy.'

She twirls her necklace around her index finger. 'It's just common sense. The problem with Cyril is that he goes off on tangents. He can be a bit much, especially in the morning. Can I get you a coffee?'

'I'm good. By the way, Seamus said to say hello.'

'Did he now?' Her eyes sparkle. 'That Irish prick barely shows his face over here lately. Tell him to come say hello himself sometime. I've got a Guinness waiting.'

'Bit of a cliché, isn't it?'

She frowns. 'What is?'

'Never mind. So, you've worked here a while?'

'Ten years, give or take.'

'You like it?'

'Wouldn't be here otherwise. Bit of a conversation killer saying you work in a cemetery. But it has its upsides. And we run a pretty tight ship here in the office, despite appearances. We get a lot of phone calls, people looking for dead relatives. Sometimes I feel like telling them they've left it a bit late, but I'm more polite than that. Mostly we work with the undertakers and stonemasons, make sure everything runs smoothly. We handle the sales here too, all the paperwork that goes with it. It's a bit of a process.'

I notice the wrinkles around her eyes, and I wonder if she's older than I thought.

'Plus, we've got the mausoleums. The prime spots there are pretty exxy, the ones with a view.'

'Is that a joke?'

She shakes her head. 'Some people want only the best for their loved ones, even when they're dead. But then, there's other people who couldn't give a shit. There are graves here where the family have never even put in a headstone. Not even a wooden crucifix, nothing. I guess they figure it doesn't matter.'

'Which camp are you in?'

She shrugs. 'Somewhere in the middle. Look, you don't want to put yourself in hock for some box that'll just rot in the dirt. People overcompensate. They try to make amends. Like it actually matters. But take it from me, it only matters if it makes you feel better. It doesn't change a thing for that body in the ground. Once you're dead, you're dead.'

'You're starting to sound like Cyril.'

She arches an eyebrow. 'And you're sounding a bit too smart to be a shearer.'

I feel the blood rush to my face.

'Not sure about that.'

She smiles. 'Oh, by the way, I forgot to mention. Someone called this morning. Someone looking for you.'

My throat goes tight.

'For me?'

'Yeah.'

'Who?'

'Didn't say.'

'What did you tell them?'

'I said I didn't know who they were talking about. You're off the books, remember?' She frowns. 'Who do you reckon it'd be?'

I grip the edge of the counter.

Ali the Turk.

Could Len have told him?

'No-one knows I'm here. Except one bloke, maybe.'

'Who?'

'Just a friend.'

She nods. 'Must've been him, then.'

If Ali knows I'm here, I'll need to leave. I'll call the hostel later, see what Len knows.

•

On the walk back to the shed, at the northern end of Entrance Avenue, I notice a dark stone memorial, adorned with artificial flowers. More flowers than any of the graves I've seen. Two etched portraits are at its centre. I recognise the face straight away.

In Evergreen Memory of Elvis Aron Presley
Born Tupelo, Mississippi 8-1-1935
Died Memphis, Tennessee 16-8-1977

'He never come here, you know.'

I look up and see a woman standing beside a grave on the opposite side of the road. She's very short, dressed in black.

'Who?' I say. 'Elvis?'

'*Si.* He never even come to this country. So I don't know why they waste money on this rubbish.'

She leans down and rearranges some faded plastic flowers. I look at the grave she's tending. Black granite, gold leaf lettering.

Vittorio Marchigiano
Born in Ascoli Piceno, Italy, in 1935. Died in 2005.
Beloved husband of Rita, devoted father to Roberto and
Claudia.
Forever In Our Hearts

A framed, sun-faded ceramic photo looks out. Vittorio wears a suit jacket and tie, a pink flower in his pocket. Must be a wedding day, maybe for Roberto or Claudia. He's almost completely bald, his eyes lit up with a wide grin.

'Your husband?'

'*Si.*'

'You're Rita then?'

'*Si. Piacere.*' She looks up at me and squints through gold-rimmed glasses. '*Come ti chiami?*'

'Tom.'

'Tommaso?'

'Just Tom.'

'*Di dove sei?*'

'*Scusa, non parlo Italiano. Parlo Inglese?*'

'*Si*, but not so good. Why you no speak Italian? You Italian, no?'

I look away, take a deep breath in and out.

'No.'

'*Vero?*'

'Of course I'm sure.'

'*Greco?*'

I shake my head. 'What happened to your husband?'

'Ah, *mannaggia*. He get the *cancro*, you know?'

'Cancer?'

'*Si*. I thought you no speak Italian.'

'*Poco poco*. So, you come here a lot?'

She sighs. 'Most day, if my hip no cause me trouble. They want to give me the hip replacement at the St Vincent's, but I no want. You know these doctors, they like the butchers sometimes. Like with my Vito. He had a tumour in his lung. Oh, they say it's no problem. Oh, they say they do this operation all the time. Routine, they say. Then, he have big stroke while they operate. He never wake up.'

'*Mi dispiace.*'

'*Grazie.* So, you visit someone too?'

'I work here.'

'You dig the grave?'

I nod. 'It's only my second day. I'm helping out for a while, until they hire someone permanent.'

'So you know Cyril?'

'Sort of.'

She smiles. 'He's a little rough around the edge, but a good heart, you know? He even bring roses here, for Vito, every year on his birthday. After he die, I used to bring flowers from the florist once a week, but too expensive. And in summer, they die too quick. So now, the plastic one. Apart from his birthday, and on the other day. He a good man, Cyril. And he no have easy life.'

'No?'

She frowns. 'But why you want to work in a cemetery?'

'I guess I like being outside.'

She nods. 'My Vito, he same. He like to work outdoors, with his hands.' She smiles again, her eyes brighten. 'They used to say he had a golden touch, you know? He could fix anything. He was builder, concreter, bricklayer, you name. He had a good business too, but then he got sick.'

'Must've been tough.'

She takes a deep breath. 'Ah, what can you do? This is a part of life. You still young, but life get very hard when you get old. And I know it make no difference to come here now, but it make me feel better. Make him feel closer. You understand?'

'I think so.'

'I talk to him, tell him what's happening in the world. He like to talk about politics, about the news. But our kids, they no come much anymore. They too busy with their kids, work. But for me, I feel bad if I no come. He was good to me, Vito. He taught me everything when we come over, even how to speak English. You know the first words he taught me?'

I shake my head.

She smiles. '"Have you got a job for me?" So, I went to the woman's hospital, the laundry there, and they give me job. The only English I knew. We have good life together, you know. Two kids, lots of grandkids. But now, just me on my own. So it give me something to do.'

I look up the road.

'I'd better get back to it.'

She nods. 'Say *ciao* to Cyril for me, okay.'

'I will.'

As I head toward the shed, I notice the small white gravestone of a young boy. A carved marble lamb his companion.

In Loving Memory of Georgie Day
Beloved only son of E & N Day
Killed at Newport Shops by injuries inflicted with compressed air
21ˢᵗ May 1921
Aged 15 ½ years

The poor kid.

I reach into my pocket and give my lucky charm a squeeze.

Even if she guessed I was Italian, that's all she knows.

She doesn't know anything else.

Three

We spend the rest of the morning getting the first gravesite ready for the burial. It's the first one we dug yesterday, in the Catholic section. We start by laying boards at each end of the grave, then two lengths of galvanised steel down each side.

'Just to give a good footing for when they lower the coffin,' Cyril says. 'Last thing you want is anyone slipping in there, especially when it's wet.'

'Has that happened?'

He nods. 'Once or twice. Ideally the undertaker will use the lowering machine, if there's enough room. Takes out the human error. But this one is a bit tight, so it'll have to be done by hand. Sometimes we get a Muslim funeral, and those ones are even more of a hassle. We have to dig the grave so their right side is perpendicular to Mecca. Plus, we have to shore up the sides, because they carry the body down by hand. No coffin or nothing, just wrapped in a shroud. She's quite a scene. They usually fill it in afterward themselves too. Luckily, we don't get too many of those. They're mostly out at Fawkner.'

We tidy up around the grave, make it as presentable as possible. Seamus rolls three strips of synthetic grass over the pile of dirt.

'In a perfect world, you'd have the dirt well out of sight,' he says. 'You can do that in country cemeteries, but it's too difficult in a place like this. There's not enough room to manoeuvre, and the clay makes a hell of a mess, especially when it's wet. The less you move it around, the better.'

In the next row over, closer to the fence, I notice maybe a dozen identical headstones, side by side. Some are blank. Seamus sees me looking.

'Those ones are reserved for the nuns,' he says. 'The church owns a fair chunk of real estate in this section.'

Cyril dusts his hands on the front of his pants.

'Think we're pretty much done. Me and Seamus will wait at the office until showtime, so you rack off back to the shed. Come over at about quarter to twelve, once everyone's gone, and then we'll fill her in. We'll break for lunch after. Next burial is at two, so we'll need to get that one ready as well.'

I walk slowly back toward the shed. The sun is warm, and I take off my jumper. It's quiet, just the faintest sound of traffic in the distance. Almost like being in the country. The slow call of crows, the wind through the trees.

How long has it been? Nearly ten years?

It was mostly a good place to grow up. Yabbying, fishing, hanging out with my best mate. School wasn't great, though. And life at home was shithouse when my father was around. As the years passed, the town seemed to close in around me. The chances to leave got fewer, and my whole world seemed to shrink.

I'd had my chance, but left it too late.

A currawong lands on top of a large gravestone next to the road, dressed in its shiny black and white plumage. It turns its head sideways, watches me pass with one yellow eye. A mynah swoops in, shrieking, tries to frighten the currawong away. Another currawong arrives, swoops the mynah. Both currawongs see it off.

I wonder if the town has changed much. I doubt it. Truth is, I can't imagine I'll ever go back. Too many people will remember me, what I did.

Towns like that never change. They never forget.

•

I wait in the shed until I see the last car go out the gate and onto Macpherson Street. It hadn't been a big funeral from what I could tell. Maybe six or seven cars, including the long silver hearse that led the procession.

At the burial site, Seamus sits on the ledger stone of a neighbouring grave, holding a shovel.

'Where's Cyril?' I say.

'Gone to get lunch. Usually shouts us on a burial day. Bit of a tradition. There's a little cafe over the road on Lygon Street, nothing fancy.' He stands up. 'You good to go?'

He hands me the shovel.

'There isn't much to it. It's a bit less complicated than the excavation. We'll use the Wacker for most of it, then clean up around it as best we can.'

I look down inside the grave. There's a dark, timber coffin with silver handles. Maybe a dozen red roses are scattered on top.

I remember my father's funeral, how light his coffin felt. My mum's face, etched in grief, as he was lowered into the earth.

Seamus shakes his head. 'Bloody cost a fortune, these things, just to rot in the ground. Some of those funeral homes are thieves, plain and simple. They push people into the top of the range, show them all the glossy brochures. The big corporate ones, especially. Some joints even push these flash ones for people getting cremated, which is just completely crooked. May as well set fire to five grand.'

'What would you want?' I say. 'When you die?'

He shrugs. 'Couldn't give a shit. Cremate me, then flush my ashes down the toilet for all I care. I'll never understand these people who leave elaborate instructions. Some even say the songs they want played at the service, what type of flowers, who gets to give a eulogy. They don't realise it isn't about them anymore.'

'Many people show up to this one?'

'About twenty. Solid turnout for an old bloke.'

'How old?'

'Eighty-four. If I make it that far, I reckon I'll be pretty happy to check out. Your body's fucked, everything hurts, most people you love are probably dead.'

'You're a real ray of sunshine.'

He grins. 'This place does it to you. All the family looked pretty distraught, though. The grandkids especially. Went pretty smooth at our end. The burials are usually over pretty quick, unless there's a full graveside service. The whole scene is pretty brutal for the family, watching that coffin go down. So the quicker it's over, the better. This wasn't a religious one, thank Christ. Just the bloke from the funeral home.'

'You're not religious then?'

He shakes his head. 'Raised Catholic, went to mass every Sunday, confession and all that. But the church fucked a lot of people back home. Literally. Here too, I'm told.'

I nod, stare into the grave.

It wasn't just the church, though. There were other people too.

Seamus scratches at his cheek. 'Aside from any of that, I don't like what they preach. Too much guilt, too much stuff about sin. Even in the funeral services. How we all need to beg for forgiveness to get into heaven. Fuck that for a joke. Life's hard enough without being told we're doing it wrong.'

He climbs up into the Wacker, starts it up.

'I'll get most of it done with this bastard, then you do the remainder with the shovel. Pretty easy.'

I roll up the fake turf, then watch as Seamus scoops the clay and soil, swings around and dumps it inside the grave with a thump. After a few scoops, I look inside and see the coffin is mostly covered. I wonder how long it'll be before it starts to rot.

I've never really thought about my own funeral, what I would want. Whether anyone would come.

Seamus fills the grave to ground level, but there's still a big pile of clay remaining.

'What about all this?'

'We pile it on top,' he says. 'It'll take a while to settle, because of all the air in it, but you can't compact it. Like I said, it risks breaking the coffin.'

He scoops up most of what's left, leaves the remnants for me to deal with. He cuts the motor on the Wacker.

'It'll look a right fucking mess for a while. A lot of families complain to the office, but there's not much we can do. People have unreasonable expectations. If you don't want any mess, you should get cremated.'

'How long til they do the headstone?'

He whistles. 'Rarely less than twelve months. Sometimes longer. Sometimes never.'

I start shovelling the dirt.

'They've got long lead times. If they get the stone from China, it can take a while. And it can cost a fucking fortune. A lot of families can't afford it, or they get in nasty fights about who's paying for what. Some people do little homemade jobs in the meantime, but sometimes the meantime goes on forever. They're meant to get approval from the office for the design, but we turn a blind eye. They do little wooden crucifixes and the like. I prefer those to the big shiny ones. More personal.'

'You boys done yet?'

I look up and see Cyril walking toward us, along a narrow path between two rows of graves. He's got two paper bags, plus some cans of soft drink in a plastic bag. I can smell the pastry. My stomach rumbles.

Seamus climbs out of the Wacker. 'What'd you get us?'

'Beef burgundy for you, chicken curry for the new boy. Already scoffed my pastie.' He eyes me. 'I'm vegetarian, so I don't touch the meat.'

'How come?'

Seamus sighs. 'Just for fucking once, I'd like to eat in peace.'

'I'll give you the abridged version. I used to eat meat, but a lot of what I read made me realise it's unethical. That Peter Singer bloke, especially. We have this idea that we're so much better than all the other animals, and they're not intelligent. And somehow that means we can do what we like. But we barely understand how our own brains work, let alone animals.

'When you think about it, we humans are pretty fucking stupid. I mean, look at what we're doing to the planet. Animals don't live like that. And I'd bet you anything that most animals live happier lives than we do. I mean, most people I know are pretty fucking miserable. Or in denial that they're pretty fucking miserable.'

Seamus takes a bite of his pie. 'This is delicious. You can't tell me you wouldn't like a bite.'

He shakes his head. 'Animals deserve our respect.'

'What about cats?' I say.

'Well, that's different. I mean, it's not their fault, but the way we've introduced them into habitats is criminal.'

I try to eat my pie slowly, to make it last. It's hot and delicious. I crack my can of lemonade, take a sip.

'I met Rita this morning,' I say. 'An Italian lady over near the Elvis memorial. She said she knows you, to say hello.'

Cyril shakes his head. 'Poor woman. After her husband died, she came here every day for the next two years. A lot of the Italians are like that. Could be the Catholic thing, but I think there's more to it. Family is their whole life, so when the inevitable happens, they seem to struggle more than most. But just because someone's gone, doesn't mean you stop having a relationship with them. They're still a part of your life. You'll get to know a few of the old Italian ladies, I'd say. Greeks too.'

He checks his watch.

'Righto. We've got about an hour to the next burial, so me and Seamus will get her ready. Same deal, Tom. You fuck off back to the shed for now. Come over at about two thirty and we'll fill her in. We've got another burial on Thursday, but we can get that ready tomorrow.'

I swallow the last of my pie. I feel like another one.

'Thanks for lunch,' I say.

Seamus gives me a look.

'No such thing as a free one, you know.'

•

Back in the shed, I sit on the bench and wait. It's about another hour until I have to go back. I kick off my boots and lie down. My back still aches, my right knee too. I'll need to blow up the air mattress at some point, but that can wait. I close my eyes and let the fatigue wash over me.

I'm nearly asleep when I'm jolted by a loud ringing. For a split second, I think I'm back in jail. I sit up, spot the phone on the back wall.

I go to answer, hesitate.

It rings twice more, stops.

I'd thought I'd do it later, maybe after Cyril and Seamus had left. I'd find a payphone somewhere, make the call. But now, the temptation is too great.

But maybe she doesn't live there anymore. Maybe she and Derek got a new place.

It rings three times.

'Hello?'

Her voice. The first time in so long.

'Hello? Who's calling?'

'It's me.'

Soft breath, in and out.

'I . . . Tom. I didn't realise. It's good to hear your voice.'

'Yours too.'

'How come they didn't—'

'I'm out. It's just been a couple of days. I hope I'm not—'

'Oh . . . that's great. It's just . . . it's been so long.'

'I know.'

'Where are you now?'

I look around the shed.

'At a mate's place. Just a short-term thing, until I can afford somewhere to rent. How have you been?'

'Good. Busy, you know. Working a lot. But I'm happy you're out, Tom. Must be a relief.'

'Yeah. Listen, I was thinking—'

'Um, look, I can't talk right now. I just heard the car pull up and—'

My heart sinks.

'Is it Derek?'

'I don't think . . . I'm not sure he'd like us talking.'

I swallow. 'Can I call again sometime?'

'I . . . I'd better go.'

'How about tomorrow?'

'Ah . . . maybe.'

'C'mon. Please.'

She sighs. 'Okay.'

'What time?'

'About three o'clock. Listen, I have to go.'

'I've really missed you.'

'I . . . bye, Tom.'

I listen to the beep as the line goes dead.

My heart is beating hard in my chest, my face is hot.

It was so good to hear her voice.

•

After the second burial, we have beers back at the shed. This time, Seamus sticks around.

He takes a deep drink, eyes me.

'So, what's your story?'

'What do you mean?'

'Dunno. You just seem different.'

I shrug.

Cyril sculls his can, lets out a burp. 'I gotta make a move. Trivia night at my local. We're on a winning streak.'

He crushes his can, tosses it in the bin.

'See you tomorrow, boys. Don't forget we've got that grave to get ready. We'll do it in the morning, then some gardening in the afternoon.' He eyes Seamus. 'By the way, it might be a special.'

Seamus nods. 'All good.'

'I'll know more later.'

'Righto.'

Cyril heads out through the roller door.

'What's a special?' I say.

Seamus shakes his head. 'Just a grave we need to take a bit more care with. Anyway, how'd you find it today?'

I shrug. 'Pretty straightforward.'

'We've been lucky with the weather, and we haven't run into any major roots. This job isn't rocket science, as long as you can get along with Cyril.'

'He seems alright. Just likes a chat.'

He nods. 'Bit of an odd one, but a good man to keep on side. If he's got your back, he'll always look out for you. Like a couple of years ago, for instance. I got myself in the shit and owed some money. They were some pretty shady characters, you know.'

'What happened?'

He shrugs. 'I was betting on the horses, mainly. Some loan sharks got me, then they wanted their pound of flesh. Anyway, Cyril helped me out.'

'He loaned you the cash?'

'Nah, he just had some connections. Some people who could make it go away.'

'What sort of people?'

He shakes his head. 'It's not important. But he's the sort of bloke you can rely on if you're ever in a bind. That said, he expects loyalty. And if you lose his trust, he'll make your life pretty difficult.'

'Is that what happened to Kev?'

He rolls his eyes.

'That's a whole other story, but it was mostly about Emily. That girl he met.'

'Cyril said her name was Eleanor.'

'Might've been.' He takes a sip of his beer. 'You remind me a bit of Kev, actually. Bit of a lone wolf, bit of a past, too.' He cuts his eyes at me. 'Cyril said you dumped a body, is that right?'

I nod. 'A long time ago.'

'What happened?'

'There was this bloke who . . . well, he was pretty bad news. My mate killed him.'

'How'd he do it?'

'Violently.'

'You were there?'

The crack of bone, the spray of blood.

'It was a spur of the moment thing. But he had it coming.'

'So, you helped get rid of him?'

'Yep.'

'What did you do?'

Swing the axe, harder this time.

My eye starts to twitch.

'I'd rather not talk about it.'

He takes another drink. 'Fair enough. But you got found out, obviously.'

I nod. 'Someone found the body. It was years later, but it got traced back to us.'

'Bummer.'

'Yeah, bummer.'

Seamus finishes the last of his beer. He stands up, tosses the can toward the bin, but misses. It rattles noisily across the concrete floor.

'I'm gonna head off.'

I watch through the roller door as Seamus cycles out through the gate, his helmet dangling from his handlebars.

It's the same story I've told plenty of times over the years. Truth is, I feel increasingly distant from what happened. There isn't the same flood of guilt and shame that once charged through me.

The kid who did it was a different person, or at least a different version of who I am now.

I could never do something like that again.

I finish my beer as slowly as I can.

•

Cyril had brought me six tins of baked beans, six cans of tinned spaghetti, and four packets of two minute-noodles. I opt for the spaghetti, then turn on the radio in the kitchen. It's tuned to some jazz station. It's soft and mellow.

As my dinner warms up in the microwave, I check my front pocket. I take out the twenty-dollar note. I only had two jobs before I went inside. Neither were great, and I wasn't great at either.

If I can stick around a few weeks, I should have enough for the bus to Brisbane, enough for a place to stay. Not for long, and definitely nowhere flash, but still.

After dinner, I have a long, hot shower. It's the first one since the hostel, and the water feels good on my skin. Outside, the light is beginning to fade.

I decide to blow up the air mattress. It takes longer than I expect, and my lungs burn. Once I recover, I lay down to test it. It's squeaky and uncomfortable, but so much better than the bench.

I call directory assistance and get the number for the hostel. If Len's told Ali that I'm at the cemetery, I'll need to make a move. Maybe head up to Brisbane a bit sooner. At the very least, I'll need to keep an eye out.

It takes a few rings, but a man answers. It could be the same one who worked the counter, the one with the beard, but I can't tell for sure.

'I was just looking for Len.'

'Who?'

'Len. The old bloke on the second floor. I don't know his surname.'

'Oh, you mean Lenny. Are you a family member?'

'Just a friend. I only need to speak to him for a minute.'

'No chance of that, I'm afraid.'

'Why not?'

'He's gone.'

'Did he leave a number?'

'I doubt it. And if he did, he wouldn't have much to say.'

'What do you mean?'

'No-one can speak to him, mate. He's dead.'

Four

I'm woken by the roller door sliding up. I squint as the morning light floods inside.

Cyril stands over me.

'Jesus, mate. You're worse than a teenager.'

Lina runs over, licks my face. I get up from the air mattress, sit on the bench, give her a pat.

'What time is it?'

'Seven o'clock. So a bit of a sleep-in.'

He walks past me and into the kitchen. I hear him fill the kettle.

'Coffee?'

'Yeah, thanks.'

My back still aches a little, but not as badly. I pull on my jeans, a jumper, then go to the toilet and take a piss. I splash some water on my face, through my hair. I look at myself in the mirror. I need a shave. Maybe later.

When I come back out, Cyril is sitting on the bench. He passes me a mug of milky coffee.

'How'd you sleep?'

'Better,' I lie.

He raises his mug. 'Cheers to that.'

My thoughts return to Len. I wonder what happened, how he died. When I asked the bloke at the hostel, I couldn't get a straight answer.

He couldn't have gone downhill so fast with the cancer, surely. He seemed fine when I last saw him.

It might've been Ali.

When Krystal told him I wasn't here, he might've figured Len had lied to him.

As we quietly sip our coffees, Seamus pulls up on his bike. Cyril taps his watch.

'Ten minutes? Big fucking deal.'

'Punctuality is everything, as you know, Seamus. Setting a bad example for the new boy.'

He takes off his helmet, wheels his bike against the inside wall of the shed.

'You win trivia?' he says.

Cyril shakes his head. 'One of the other teams had a ring-in. Some old prick who swallowed some encyclopaedias. Plus, there were lots of geography questions and pop culture, neither of which are our strong suit. We came second, though. Won a few free jugs.'

Seamus goes into the kitchen. I can hear him making a coffee. Cyril gives me a nudge.

'You better get some breakfast. I've got a few jobs for you this morning.'

I head out back and make some toast. I smear on some margarine, Vegemite. Seamus watches, shakes his head.

'You lather it on pretty thick.'

'It's how I like it.'

'You'll end up with high cholesterol. It's a killer, you know.'

When we come back out, Cyril has shifted my air mattress against the wall, folded up my bedding.

'All part of the service,' he says. 'After you've had your breakfast, there's some cleaning up I'd like you to do. Around near the Burke and Wills memorial. A bit of debris from the storm we had a couple of weeks back. A few big branches down on the road. We don't get much traffic around there, but it'd be good to give it a tidy up.'

'Where's the memorial?'

'Not far from the office. Just head over there and Krystal can give you directions. Me and Lance Armstrong here will handle that grave we need to dig.'

Seamus takes a sip of his coffee.

'Where's the grave?' he says.

'Near the east gate, which should make it easier for later.'

•

When I get to the office, Krystal is pulling up in her hatchback. She climbs out of the car, slams the door shut. She's wearing high heels, shiny red leather. A short skirt that looks a little too tight.

She opens the passenger side, picks up a handbag. It looks expensive, in brown and gold leather, with a thick gold chain dangling from one side.

She looks a bit startled to see me.

'Still here, then?'

'Seems that way.'

'Well, we've got a busy week coming up.' She loops her handbag over her shoulder. 'But what brings you here so early?'

I tell her about the clean-up job, that I need directions.

She rolls her eyes. 'Sounds like they're trying to keep you busy. What are those two up to?'

'Digging the grave for tomorrow.'

'Glad to hear it. It's just a single, so it shouldn't take them long.' She frowns. 'Has Cyril been treating you okay?'

I nod.

'He's a bit of a rough diamond, but good at his job. I'm surprised you've stayed in touch with him, given his colourful past.' She tilts her head toward the office. 'Got time for a coffee?'

'Maybe later,' I say. 'I better get started.'

She locks her car with an electronic beep. 'Suit yourself. Just head over to where that path starts, past the mausoleum on the right, then follow the path around to the left. It's only a few minutes' walk. You can't miss it, a great big obelisk type thing, made out of granite. If you get lost, just carve your name and where you were headed into a tree. We'll find you.'

'Hilarious.'

She shakes her head. 'Those poor souls, lost out there in the desert like that. Not sure that big memorial does them much good.'

'Do people ever visit?'

She heads toward the office. 'We get school groups, a few history buffs. There's a lot of famous people in here, though. Prime ministers, sports people, actors, criminals, you name it. Death is the great leveller. We all become neighbours, whether we like it or not.'

'You're sounding like Cyril again.'

She smiles. 'That's really quite insulting.'

'I'd better go clean up that mess.'

She gives me a look. 'Yeah, you better.'

'By the way, that bloke who rang yesterday. How did he sound?'

'I dunno, just like some bloke.'

'That's helpful.'

She frowns. 'Pretty well spoken, I guess.'

'How old?'

'Hard to tell over the phone, you know. In his forties, maybe?'

That doesn't sound like Ali.

'Listen, I'd better go open up. If you get to the Jewish area then you've gone too far. But you can always come back if you need.' She smiles. 'Otherwise, I might see you for that coffee.'

•

That afternoon, we do some weeding on the verge of North Avenue, the main road that bisects the cemetery. Lina lies on her back in the gutter, warming her belly in the sun.

'We always do the prominent areas first,' Seamus says. 'The parts where people drive and walk through the most. There just isn't enough time to do the whole lot.'

I think of the older section near Lygon Street that looks almost completely abandoned. Paths cracked, graves uprooted, weeds everywhere.

'We try to keep up appearances,' Cyril says. 'Especially when we get complaints. But some areas are beyond redemption. Back in the Depression, a lot of graves got vandalised, ornaments stolen. They didn't know what to do with the place, so it got locked up and was made into a wildlife sanctuary. Eventually it got cleaned up, but by the sixties they let it go to ruin again. Run pretty badly, so they say. They were doing all sorts of crooked shit right up until the seventies, even reusing some of the existing plots.'

'Where people were already buried?'

He nods. 'They thought they could make some extra cash by recycling. Resold hundreds that were already occupied, mostly pauper's graves. Sold most of them to the Italians and Greeks, apparently. So you can see why we never know what we'll find when we start digging. Story goes they were even reselling some of the funeral wreaths.'

'Jesus.'

'They were on the take, every which way. That's why it's more overcrowded than it should be. They made a right mess of it.'

'What time is it?' I say.

Cyril stops his weeding, gives me a look. 'Not enjoying the history lesson?'

'I gotta call someone.'

'Who?'

'Just someone.'

He shakes his head. 'Mate, you need my permission to take a break. And I'll only give you permission if you tell me.'

I take a breath in and out.

'Just someone I used to know. From before I went inside.'

He leans on his spade, lights a cigarette. 'Well, that's a start. Let me guess, it's a woman, right? Wouldn't happen to be that bird up in Queensland?'

I stare at the ground.

He grins. 'It wasn't hard to figure that one out. Look, I don't want to get in the way of true love. There's a phone box out on Lygon Street. Just go out through the east gate.'

I'd hoped he'd let me call from the shed, but don't want to push my luck.

'What time do you need to call her?'

'Three o'clock.'

He checks his watch. 'You've got ten minutes, Romeo.'

'You got any change?'

He sighs, reaches into his pocket, flicks me a two-dollar coin.

'That's all I got. Seamus?'

He shakes his head.

I drop my spade and walk quickly through the cemetery. I go along Tenth Avenue, then take the third left down East Avenue. Not far from the gate, just a few rows back, I see a couple of witches hats. Must be the grave Cyril and Seamus dug this morning. It's covered with a big sheet of plywood, weighed down with bricks.

I go out through the gate and onto Lygon Street. A tram rushes past heading north, cars and trucks too. I spot the phone box on the opposite side of the street, outside a block of flats.

I drop the two-dollar coin into the slot, hold the phone hard against my ear. I wonder how long it will give me to Brisbane. The traffic is noisy, but I hear the click as the call connects.

'Hello?'

'It's me.'

'Listen, I haven't got long.'

'I thought you said—'

'I know, but it's tricky.'

'I can call some other time if—'

'No, it's alright.'

'It's good to hear your voice again.'

A pause. Too long.

'Yours too.'

'So, how's work going?'

'It's good. Just busy. I'm never gonna get rich doing bar work, you know. But how about you? Are you looking for work, or . . .'

'I've already found something.'

'That's great.'

'Just some gardening, nothing too exciting.'

'Whereabouts?'

I hesitate.

'A cemetery. It's just a short-term thing.'

'That's good, Tom. A little morbid, but good.'

'Not very glamorous, I know.'

'I'm having trouble hearing you.'

'I'm at a payphone. Listen, I don't know how long I've got. I only put in a couple of dollars and . . . anyway, I'm saving some money. From the job, I mean. And I was thinking maybe I could come up and visit. I could get a bus and come up for a few days. I've never been to Brisbane before and—'

'Um, I don't know. Now might not be the best time. Just with work and everything.'

'I can wait until you get some time off or—'

'Listen, I'm just not sure it's the best idea. It's been such a long time, you know?'

There's a sinking feeling in my stomach, my chest.

'But that's why I want to see you.'

'I don't think . . .' she sighs. 'I mean, I think you should just try to get settled first, to adjust. You've been inside a long time. I don't want you to spend all your money and—'

'But I've been looking forward to it.'

'I just don't think it's a good idea right now.'

'When then?'

She hesitates. 'I'm not sure.'

My face feels like it's burning.

'Is it because of Derek?'

'No, not because of that. There's just been a lot of water under the bridge.'

'But you said in your letter . . . you said I could come up and see you.'

'I know. It's just . . . listen, I'd better go.'

'Can I call you again?'

'I . . . I'm not sure. Let's just leave it for a week or two, okay? See how you feel then.'

'But—'

'I've gotta go, Tom. Sorry.'

The phone line clicks, then goes dead. I keep holding the phone against my ear.

My throat hurts, my chest.

I hang up the phone.

•

When I get back to Cyril and Seamus, they've already started packing up the tools, loading them onto the four-wheeler. Lina sees me coming and runs to my side, tail wagging. I give her a scratch.

Cyril eyes me. 'Why the long face?'

'Nothing.'

'Girl trouble?'

I shrug.

He shakes his head. 'Don't let it get you down. Plenty more fish and all that. Besides, you'd be better off with a dog. Not as much fun, maybe, but a lot less complication.'

We pack up the rest of the gear, head back to the shed. Once we've put away the tools, Cyril tells me and Seamus to knock off for the day. He attaches a leash to Lina's collar.

'Gotta take this one to the vet,' he says. 'She costs me a fucking fortune. Skin conditions, allergies, you name it.'

I sit down on the bench. Even though I haven't done much work, I feel exhausted.

'Catch you both tomorrow,' Seamus says. He picks up his bike from against the wall. 'What time's that burial again?'

'Eleven,' Cyril says. He gives my shoulder a squeeze as he passes, slips me fifty bucks.

'Go out for a walk, get yourself some beers. Try not to dwell on things so much. It's still early days for you, and it's no good sitting here stewing. Things will get easier, trust me.'

I look up at him and nod.

'I'll be better tomorrow,' I say.

He slaps me on the back. 'That's the way. Onward and upward.'

•

After a shower and a shave, I decide to take Cyril's advice. I walk out of the north gate, turn left toward Princes Park.

I walk along the path, keep my head down as people pass. Someone's dog, off leash, runs up and jumps on my leg. A white fluffy thing, some sort of terrier.

'Sorry!'

I look up as a woman approaches, dressed in olive Lycra tights. A white t-shirt. She flashes me a smile.

'That's okay,' I say. 'What's her name?'

'*His* name. Felix.'

I give the dog a pat.

The woman continues past me, the dog follows.

'Have a nice day,' she says.

Once I get to Princes Park, I decide to do a loop around the grandstand. I remember this is where Carlton used to play. Joggers run past, mothers with prams, people walking dogs.

Cyril was right. It feels good to be out of the cemetery and in the sun.

I try my best not to think of the phone call, but my thoughts keep returning to what she said, how she sounded. She seemed removed, distant.

But maybe I'm misreading things. It was pretty unrealistic to think she'd just welcome me back after so many years. I can't expect her to drop everything.

I'll try to focus on the work, save as much as I can, then call her in a few weeks. If she sees I've got my shit together, maybe she'll change her mind. She probably just needs more time.

Around the other side of the grandstand, nearer to Royal Parade, I see someone lying under a tree, wrapped in a black sleeping bag. They have the hood pulled over their head, their face obscured. Trams ding past on the road, peak hour traffic, bikes racing home.

I head back toward the cemetery.

•

It's baked beans again, washed down with two cans of VB I bought from a bottle shop on Lygon Street. I feel better after the beers.

I sit on a stool in the kitchen with the radio on, listening to some old-timey jazz. I like the sound of it, gravelly and raw. It's already dark outside, but still too early for sleep. I look out the window, the cemetery silvered by moonlight.

I decide to take a walk.

Outside, the air is cooler than I expected. I pull my jacket in, zip it up. I decide to go left down the hill, along Fourteenth Avenue. I'll do a loop, follow the road around toward the gatehouse, then head back. That should tire me out, take my mind off things.

I look up at the night sky and try to find the Milky Way, but the stars are nowhere near as bright as in the country. The half-moon bathes the graves in soft grey light, the road beside like a dark, curving river. In the distance, I can hear the hum of traffic. I look ahead to the city skyline, the blinking red and yellow lights.

On my left, there's a section of Chinese graves in the middle of a Catholic area. I'd noticed it earlier, concreted and ringed off with a chain fence. Its graves are smaller, more humble than its neighbours. Only the names of the dead. No dates, no florid declarations.

I sense movement, a presence. My heart beats hard in my chest. I stop and look up the narrow road diverging at my right. At first, I don't recognise it.

Then, I remember.

A woollen jumper my mum knitted, a thick black coat that didn't quite fit. Light rain falling. My father beside me, with the rifle at his side.

'Look,' he whispered. '*Volpe.*'

The fox looked at us, quizzical, maybe thirty metres away. It stood still, waiting for movement.

'Are you going to shoot him?' I said.

My father smiled, gave my shoulder a squeeze. I looked up as the fox ran over a small hill and out of sight.

'He is very wise, the fox.'

I smile at the memory. I open my eyes and watch the fox trot quickly away through the headstones. I reach into my pocket, give my rabbit's foot a squeeze.

I don't think of my father much these days, and the years have clouded the memories. No photos, no clear recollection. His appearance reduced to a faded outline. The memory of a memory, each time further removed.

But when I close my eyes sometimes, I can feel his presence. His solidity, his earthiness, his heavy hand on my shoulder. The sound of the front door creaking open, his footsteps down the hallway.

I spot the east gate, down a pathway to my left. I look down the path and out to Lygon Street. I see bright car headlights flashing past. It's the same gate I came through when I first arrived. It's locked now, but I've seen gaps in the fence nearby, places where the iron posts have broken or come loose, never repaired or replaced.

A quick detour won't hurt.

I head off the road and walk carefully along the concrete path. The graves here are old and very humble, much smaller than other parts, the footpath cracked and uneven. It's too dark to make out any inscriptions on the headstones, even with the yellow glow of streetlights from outside. I'm guessing the real estate near the fence wasn't as sought after as further up the hill. The places with better views of the city, the Dandenongs.

To my left, I spot the grave Cyril and Seamus dug earlier.

The special.

Two witches hats keep vigil ahead of the burial tomorrow, a third is knocked over.

I pick it up, then position it on a corner of the plywood. I see the pile of dirt and clay a few rows back, a couple of shovels beside. The pile looks bigger than I expected.

I'm sure Krystal said it was a single, though.

I take the witches hats off the plywood, shift the bricks. I move slowly in the gloom, careful not to trip and lose my footing. The traffic rushes past outside, a tram passes, then another soon after.

I move around the other side, take one corner of the plywood, lift it slowly from the grave. I look down into the hole, its inky blackness.

It's hard to be completely sure in the dark, but it looks much deeper than the single we dug in the Catholic section.

I put the plywood back in place, shift the bricks on top. I put the witches hats back in each corner.

Why would they dig it deeper?

Maybe it's something to do with the foundations. Maybe it's a bigger headstone and it needs deeper footings. Maybe that's what they meant when they said it was a special.

I suddenly get a strange feeling, as though I'm being watched. I turn around quickly, but there's no-one there.

The breeze picks up again from the south, cool on my skin.

Maybe it was the fox. Maybe it was my imagination.

I decide to head back to the shed.

Five

Next morning, I'm woken again by the roller door.

I sit up, squint at the early morning light.

'See?' Cyril says. 'What did I tell you?'

Seamus stands beside him. He's holding a shovel.

I rub my eyes. 'What time is it?'

Seamus leans his shovel against the wall. 'Six thirty.'

'Why so early?'

Cyril takes off his jacket, slings it onto the bench.

'Me and the Irishman had a couple of things to do, to get a head start on the day.'

He heads toward the kitchen.

I climb out of bed, pull on my jeans.

Seamus sits on the bench. 'Just some stuff Krystal asked us to sort out before we get too busy. Happens from time to time.'

I pull on my socks and boots, stifle a yawn. 'What time's the burial?'

'Eleven. Krystal says it's some lady in her sixties. We'll need your help getting the gravesite ready. Same routine. Then you can help fill it in.'

I remember what I saw last night, how deep the grave looked.

'It was a single, right?'

He scratches at his goatee. 'Yeah, that's right. So not much work.'

Cyril comes back from the kitchen with two mugs of coffee. He passes me one.

'Where's mine?' Seamus says.

'Only got two hands.'

Seamus sighs, goes out back. Cyril takes a sip of his coffee.

'How's Lina?' I say.

He shakes his head. 'Those vets see me coming from a mile away, even worse than mechanics.' He sits on the bench beside me. 'You sleeping okay on the air mattress?'

'Yeah, but I took a bit of a walk around the cemetery last night. Just to tire myself out.'

He frowns. 'Is that right?'

I blow the steam from my coffee, try to cool it.

'You didn't get spooked?'

'Nah.'

He shakes his head. 'I always say the people in here can't do you much harm. It's the ones outside you've gotta worry about.' He takes another sip. 'See anything interesting?'

For a second, I consider mentioning the grave, how deep it looked, but decide against it. I don't want him to think I was snooping around.

'Just a fox.'

He nods. 'Plenty of those around. They're pretty harmless, though. I know people say they're vermin, but to me, they've got a kind of quiet dignity.' He takes out his pack of cigarettes, lights one. 'Didn't see anything else?'

I notice a shift in tone, barely perceptible. A tightness in his voice.

'Nah, it's quiet in here at night.'

Seamus comes back from the kitchen carrying a coffee and what's left of a packet of biscuits. He places the biscuits on the bench beside me, leans back against the four-wheeler.

Cyril eyes him. 'This bloke went for a bit of a stroll last night.'

Seamus raises his eyebrows. 'Is that so?'

I nod.

'See anything exciting?'

'Like what?'

He shrugs. 'Dunno. Anybody else wandering around?'

I shake my head.

'Well, we must be doing something right then. Burying them proper-like.'

He glances at Cyril, gives him a look I can't quite read.

'So, what's the plan?' he says.

Cyril takes a deep drag of his cigarette, places his mug on the floor.

'We'll get that grave ready, obviously. Then we've got the burial. A bit of gardening this arvo, depending on how we go for time. We'll probably knock off early, seeing how we had an early start. Me and you, that is.'

I sip my coffee. It's too strong.

'Can I help with the burial this time?'

Seamus gives me a look.

'It's not exactly entertainment, you know.'

Cyril shakes his head. 'Not this one. It'll likely be a small funeral, so having three of us there is a bit heavy handed. It's not a great look for the undertakers and gravediggers to outnumber the mourners. Maybe the next one, though. I'll have to get you some new clothes, mind. Somehow, you're looking shabbier every day.'

He butts out his cigarette on the ground, swallows down the rest of his coffee.

'Righto,' he says. 'We'd better get to it.'

•

We load some tools into the back of the ute, the grave boards too, then climb inside. Cyril drives. The radio is on, and it sounds like it might be the same jazz station as in the shed. There's someone playing the piano.

As we approach the east gate, I get the feeling that something has changed. At first, I'm not sure what. But as we get closer, I realise.

The pile of dirt. It looks much smaller.

Cyril pulls up on the verge, cuts the engine. We climb out of the ute.

There's dirt on the path, footprints. Maybe they were already there last night, but there's no way I can tell for sure. I'd definitely seen two shovels, though. Pitched into the pile of dirt. Now there's only one, and it's leaning against a headstone.

They must've come here early to tidy things up. Maybe that's what Krystal asked them to do. Just to get a head start on things, like Cyril said.

Seamus unloads the boards from the back of the ute, balances them on one shoulder.

'Same deal as last time,' Cyril says. 'We'll give it a good clean, make sure it looks presentable. It's her final journey, you know. A horror show for the family, but we'll do our best to make it go smoothly.'

He fetches a roll of fake turf from the back tray, passes me a broom. He drops the roll of turf near the pile of dirt, then crouches down beside the grave. He shifts the bricks off the plywood, then takes one corner.

'You get the other side,' he says.

I lean the broom against an adjacent grave, crouch down and take the opposite corner. We lift the plywood carefully, then carry it to the ute tray. Seamus starts unrolling the turf over the pile of dirt.

Cyril passes me the broom. 'Give it a sweep around the gravesite, make sure she's nice and clean. Then we'll put the boards and the steel down.'

I go to the grave's edge, look down.

When I was inside, I quickly learned to keep a straight face. Pretending you haven't seen anything is important, if you want to survive. I start sweeping around the edge of the grave.

Maybe it was my imagination. Maybe the beers last night went to my head. It was dark, after all.

I look down again into the grave.

No, it's definitely much shallower than it was last night. The earth looks loose at the bottom too, like it's been partially filled.

That must've been what they were doing first thing.

Maybe they fucked up the depth, and Krystal set them straight. That could be it. They just didn't want me to know.

I feel my face getting hot.

'You alright?'

I look up at Cyril. He's leaning on his shovel, staring at me with his pale blue eyes.

'Yeah, I'm fine. Why?'

'You look like there's something on your mind.'

'Nah.'

'You sure about that?'

'Yeah.'

I go back to my sweeping, but I can still feel Cyril's eyes on me.

'Well, you better get on with it,' he says. 'The clock's ticking.'

•

It was the same deal as last time. I had to go back to the shed during the burial, then return to the gravesite once the mourners and undertaker had left.

Cyril is sitting on the ute's bonnet, smoking. Seamus sits behind the steering wheel with the door open.

'How was it?' I say.

Cyril clocks me, flicks his cigarette butt onto the grass.

'Not bad, only about ten or so mourners. The daughter lost her shit, but I've seen much worse. All over pretty quick.'

Cyril gets inside the Wacker, starts it up, then positions it between the pile of dirt and the grave. He starts scooping the dirt, dropping thick clumps of clay onto the coffin with a heavy thump. I look out the cemetery gate. A woman and her Dalmatian walk past on the footpath. She looks at the Wacker with wide eyes, then looks away.

Once Cyril has done most of it, I start with the shovel.

'Make sure you tamp it down a bit as you go,' he says. 'But not too hard.' He climbs out of the Wacker. 'I'm gonna go grab some lunch. You boys happy with pies again?'

We nod.

'Righto then, back in a bit.'

Once I've finished with the dirt, I sweep around the grave as best I can. It's still a bit of a mess.

'That'll do it,' Seamus says. 'Doesn't have to be perfect. We can let mother nature do the rest.'

We pack up the shovels and tools, carry them over to the ute.

'I'll just shift the Wacker,' he says.

I watch as he manoeuvres the digger between the graves and out onto the road. I lean back against the ute. The sun has broken through the clouds, and I like the warmth on my skin. The sky is big and wide here, like in the country.

Seamus cuts the motor.

'Job's right,' he says. 'Cyril can drive her back to the shed after.'

Seamus opens the passenger door, sits down with one leg outside. On his left leg, I notice the edge of a Celtic tattoo above his socks.

'What's with the tatt?'

He raises his eyebrows. 'Got it years ago, back in Ireland. Barely even notice it now. You got any?'

'Nah.'

'Weren't into the prison tatts, then?'

I shake my head. 'Not into hepatitis, either.'

We go quiet for a while. I look out the gate. I can see the cafe in the distance, over the road. I figure I'll be able to spot Cyril on his way back.

'So, what was the story with that grave?'

Straight away, I wish I hadn't said it.

He frowns. 'What do you mean?'

'You said it was a special, right?'

He crosses his arms.

'Who said it was a special?'

'You did, I think? Or Cyril?'

'You don't miss much, do you?'

'I just wondered what it means.'

He shakes his head. 'Listen, don't take this the wrong way, but sometimes it's better not to know everything. You get me?'

I shrug. 'Was just curious, that's all.'

'Yeah,' he says. 'Just curious.'

I should've kept quiet.

I spot Cyril crossing the road. He's carrying a plastic bag. He dodges between the cars, then waits for a tram to pass. He jogs through the gate and up the path.

Seamus eyes him. 'What are you all smiles about?'

'That blonde number was working, that's what.'

'Mate, she's half your age. You really think she's looking for a gravedigger as old as her father?'

Cyril lights a cigarette, passes Seamus his pie. 'You think she wants a bog Irishman instead?'

'I didn't say that. Anyway, she isn't my type.'

'That's your problem.' He passes me a pie and a can of lemonade. 'What've you boys been chatting about?'

Seamus shoots me a look.

'Nothing,' I say.

•

The Jewish section is at the southern end of the cemetery, not far from the office and main gates.

'We've had some complaints these last few weeks,' Cyril says. 'Krystal has been copping an earful, so we'll give it a spruce up.'

The graves here seem less elaborate and ornate than other parts. Many have only names and dates. Rosenblums, Meyers, and Cohens. None seem to have flowers or vases, but a few have pebbles scattered on top.

'What's with the stones?' I say.

'They reckon it helps keep their souls here on earth,' Seamus says. 'Bit selfish, in my book. They've probably got somewhere else they wanna be.'

Cyril shakes his head. 'Don't listen to this bloke. It's actually about evil spirits, keeping them out. Personally, I don't buy into any of that hocus pocus. But it's better than buying flowers that are dead in a couple of days.'

Seamus and Cyril watch as I do most of the work. I start by pulling weeds out between cracks in the concrete, then spray some Round-Up. The ache starts to return to my lower back.

'Aren't you gonna help?' I say.

Cyril sits down on a grave, lights a cigarette. 'Nah, this is all good experience. Consider it your on-the-job training, in lieu of a formal qualification. Actually, you're doing such a good job, we might just leave you to it. Our day started a bit earlier than yours, after all. Besides, I've got somewhere I need to be, and I'm sure Seamus has got better things to do.'

I give Cyril a look. He smiles, the hint of silver glinting in his teeth. He lets out a thick plume of blue smoke.

'Look, I'm feeling generous. So just finish this row and the next. Should only take you an hour or so. We'll catch you tomorrow morning.'

They head back to the road and climb into the ute. The sun has gone behind a cloud, and I'm grateful for it. I look over to the next row. It's even more weedy than this one. It will take me at least an hour, maybe two.

I hear the ute start up and then watch it go down the road. Instead of taking the turn-off toward the shed, they head left toward the office. Cyril must be checking the program for tomorrow. Or maybe Krystal promised them a beer.

I work as quickly as I can, pulling up the weeds and throwing them into a rubbish bag. It seems a pointless exercise.

The cemetery is infested with weeds and they'll be back soon enough. A honeyeater lands on a grave in the next row and watches me work.

It takes maybe an hour just to get one row done, and I need a break. I spot a garden tap a few rows away.

The water comes out warm at first, then cool. I splash some on my face, then cup my hands underneath. It's delicious. I comb the water through my hair, look back at the row still to do. My back still hurts, but I feel a little better.

'Tom.'

I turn quickly, spot a man walking toward me on the path from the road. I don't recognise him. He's maybe in his forties, balding, dressed in a blue shirt and dark pants. I hadn't heard a car pull up, so he must've come on foot.

'Sorry,' he says. 'I didn't mean to give you a start. But the girl in the office said I might find you here.'

I dry my hands on my pants.

'Do I know you?'

The man smiles. 'Not exactly, no. But I know you.'

'What's that sposed to mean?'

'Sorry, I don't mean to be obtuse.' He holds out his hand. 'The name's Neville. Neville Barton.'

I shake his hand. 'Tom.'

'Yeah, I know. So, you been doing this long?'

'The weeding?'

'Nah, this job.'

'Not really. Sorry, what's this about?'

He holds up his hands. 'My apologies. I've never been a great conversationalist, more like a bull at a gate. I'm a writer you see, so I don't get out much. Well, a journalist to be precise. At least that's what pays the bills. I'm working on a novel too, but that's a whole other story. I write for *The Argus*. Do you read it?'

'No.'

He nods. 'Probably just as well. It used to have some integrity, and people used to trust what they read. But most of it is celebrity gossip now, or media releases dressed up as news. Us old-school newsroom journos are a dying breed. The internet and social media have fucked us royally. So these days I mostly do features, and mostly about crime.'

I feel a cold trickle of sweat run down my chest.

'Given how long I've been around, it's too expensive for the bastards upstairs to make me redundant. So they give me a decent number of columns each week for some supposedly in-depth reportage. Not enough of that now, let me tell you. But don't get me started.'

'I think you already did.'

'Like I said, I don't get out much.'

'I've got a bit of work to do, so—'

'All good, all good. Non-verbal cues always seem to pass me by, or so the Mrs says. I promise I won't take much of your time. It was hard enough to find you, so I don't want to scare you off. Just half an hour, that's all I need.'

'What for?'

'Just a friendly chat. Meet me at Filou's in an hour? When you knock off? My treat.'

'Filou's?'

'The little French cafe on Lygon Street. They make beautiful pastries, I'm told. I'll even buy you a vanilla slice, if you're keen.'

There's a tightness in my throat, my chest. I take a deep breath in and out.

'How did you find me?'

He grins. 'Your old mate, Lenny.'

I shake my head. 'I barely knew him. And he's dead now, anyway.'

'Yeah, I heard. Poor bastard.'

'You know what happened?'

He nods. 'Threw himself off a multi-storey carpark, apparently. The one next door to the hostel. Pretty common move, especially since they put the suicide barriers up on the West Gate. The curse of unintended consequences, you might say.'

I shake my head. 'Poor Len.'

'Can't blame him, really. Pancreatic cancer is one of the worst, and he was doing it all alone. But before he left this mortal coil, he gave me the tip you might be here, sleeping rough. So I spoke to that girl in the office, Krystal, who gave me short shrift. But I'm nothing if not persistent. I've got a contact at the prison who told me you were in touch with some woman in Queensland, calling her pretty regular. Lucy someone.'

My breath catches in my throat.

'You spoke to her?'

He narrows his eyes. 'Took a bit of persuading, but she told me you were working here, not just sleeping rough. So, I told that Krystal that if she wasn't straight with me, I might do a piece on them hiring staff off the books. Not paying proper entitlements and all that. It was a bluff, but it seemed to get her attention.'

'What's this about?'

He smiles. 'I'll fill you in when we have a coffee.'

'Look, I've got a lot to do here.'

'How about tomorrow, then?'

I shake my head. 'I'm not sure.'

'Mate, I'm not asking the world. It's no big deal, I promise. Just a few questions. One coffee, and then I'll leave you in peace.'

I look him up and down. I get the sense he won't let it go.

'Just a coffee, then.'

His eyes light up.

'Beauty. Four pm tomorrow?'

'Okay.'

He holds out his hand. 'It's been great to finally meet you, Tom. I'll see you tomorrow.'

I watch as he walks slowly back toward the road, and I notice he has a slight limp. He must've been the bloke who came looking for me at the hostel. Maybe it wasn't Ali after all.

I go back to my weeding. The sun has gone behind a cloud, and there's a cooler southerly starting to pick up. I work as quickly as I can. A wattlebird calls from a tree nearby, but there's no answer.

There's only one thing the journo could be interested in. And it's the one thing I don't want to talk about.

The one thing I wish would go away.

Six

Next morning, when Cyril arrives, I'm making myself toast with Vegemite.

'Glad to see you're up for once.' He fills the kettle, switches it on. 'Just the two of us today. Seamus called in sick. A night on the tiles, I'd say.'

Lina runs into the kitchen, jumps on my leg. I give her a pat, take a bite of my toast, swallow it down. I'd had a rough night's sleep, my back aching, thoughts swirling about the journo and what he might want.

Why would he want to talk to me after all this time?

Cyril scoops two heaped teaspoons of coffee into his mug. 'This is why I need you around. If that bloke's off sick, which is pretty regular, I'm on my own. Hard to keep up, you know. Especially with a few burials coming up. Digging graves is a minimum two-man job. One in the Wacker, the other to spot.'

I throw Lina a piece of crust. 'We got much on today?'

He frowns. 'Got somewhere you need to be?'

I shrug. 'Just asking.'

He pours the boiling water into his mug. 'Bit of lawnmowing, that's about it. You want a coffee?'

He gets another mug out from the cupboard, makes mine with just one spoonful.

'We're not usually this busy, but it's nothing compared to the bigger cemeteries. Out at Fawkner, they do four or five burials a day. But it's mostly existing rights holders here. Makes the burials a bit tricker, the lack of space, but the trade-off is that we don't do as many. We still get a few mausoleum interments, though. We've actually got one tomorrow, but I won't need you for that.'

He tops up both coffees with milk. I add a little more to mine. I sit on the bench, while Cyril leans his weight against the Wacker.

'What happens with the interments?'

He blows the steam from his coffee. 'There isn't much to it. We take off the front plate, then the coffin gets loaded in off a trolley. We stick some wooden dowels on the shelf beforehand, so she slides in easy. You just have to make sure she's lined up straight. There's nothing worse than the sound of a coffin scraping along the side. Like nails on a blackboard, only ten times worse. There's also a couple of plugs you need to take out down the back, before you slide her in.'

'Plugs?'

He nods. 'One to drain the liquid, the other to let some air in. If you don't take those out, it can end up one hell of a soupy mess. For the ones further up the wall, the cheap ones, they usually go in off a scissor lift. There's a bit more to those, but it's manageable.'

Lina leans against my leg, looks up for a pat.

'Why are those ones cheaper?'

'The ones up top? Not at eye level, for one thing. Just like any other real estate, it's all about location.'

He sits down on the bench beside me.

'People waste a lot of money, in my book. They spend a fortune when the person's dead, probably more than they ever spent when they were alive. Sometimes we even have to get the coffins out for relocations, like if the family move overseas. It's not so bad if they're in the mausoleum, but a bitch of a job if we have to dig them out.'

I take a sip of my coffee. 'Grief does strange things to people, I spose.'

He frowns. 'Yeah, and we all see things differently. I've read a fair bit about this stuff.'

'About grief?'

'Nah, about perspective. We have this idea that we all see things in a similar way. We think there's some kind of objective reality, you know? That there's this world out there that looks, feels, and smells the same to all of us. But a lot of the science says the opposite.'

I finish my second slice of toast. I feel like another.

'We think our eyes are filming things like a movie, but that's not how it works. What we see is mostly an image created by our brain, in the visual cortex. The messages we get through our senses are just checking the image is more or less right, so we don't walk off a cliff, or out in front of a car. It's a result of evolution, natural selection.'

'No offence, but it's a bit early in the day for this.'

He smiles, the silver glints in his teeth. 'Well, take that Wacker there. We both might say it's painted yellow, but what me and you perceive as yellow might be two different things. And besides, colour doesn't really exist, right? It's just the intensity of reflected light.'

I'm reminded of another cellmate I had, an Algerian named Jamal. He was inside for drug offences, trafficking to be exact. He once argued the banana we had with our breakfast might be purple. It was hard to take him seriously after that.

I rub Lina behind her ear, and she grumbles happily. I swallow down the last of my coffee.

'I'm not sure I buy it,' I say. 'I mean, how would you really know if we see things differently?'

'Let me give you another example. This one might make more sense. Now, say there was a grave we dug. You might look at it and say it's a particular depth, and I might say it's much shallower. It depends on what we expect to see. Hypothetically, of course.'

My throat goes tight.

He knows.

Cyril smiles, lights a cigarette. He takes a deep drag.

'Well, I can see that got your attention.'

'Did Seamus say something?'

'Didn't I just say it was hypothetical?'

'But I—'

'Mate, just listen to me for a minute. Your eyes can play tricks on you sometimes, right? And we all make mistakes, you know. It's no biggie. You've been doing such a good job helping us out, and it's appreciated. And you wanna know something? Me and Seamus have been talking. If you play your cards right, that permanent job might come your way.'

'I thought it had to be advertised?'

He shakes his head. 'I can sort it easy enough with Krystal, streamline the process, so to speak. No-one wants to fuck around with interviews if there's no real need. You'd get a proper wage, good money. You could even rent your own place, have a decent bed to sleep in.'

With the extra cash I could head up to Brisbane sooner, maybe just for a weekend. I think she'd be okay with that.

'That'd be great,' I say.

He pats me on the shoulder. 'You've earned it. But I need people I can trust. You get me?'

I nod.

'I don't think I need to tell you this, but this world doesn't owe you any favours. It's brutal out there. Won't be easy for you, especially. You've got no references, no paper trail, no qualifications. It's much tougher than it used to be.'

I stare at the floor. 'I always get by.'

'Maybe. But you shouldn't look a gift horse in the mouth, either. You like working here, don't you?'

'Yeah.'

'Well, like I told you before, I trust my instincts. And I think I can rely on you to do things right.'

He takes another drag of his cigarette.

'Who knows? You could end up like me one day, in charge of things. I started out more or less like you, rose through the ranks. Mostly through attrition. The other blokes who worked here, their hearts weren't really in it. It was just a means to an end for them. But for me, this place is everything. It saved my life, to be honest. And I reckon it could save yours too. But for me to help you out, we need to be on the same page. Do we understand each other?'

'I think so.'

He smiles. 'Good lad. Oh, I nearly forgot.'

He goes outside. Lina stays at my foot, looks up at me for another pat. I hear a car door open, then slam shut. Cyril returns holding a white shopping bag, passes it to me.

'Some new clothes. Not from the op shop this time, you'll be pleased to know. There's some half decent stuff at Kmart these days.'

'Thanks.'

'Nothing fancy, but it'll make you presentable for the next burial. And one more thing.' He reaches into his pocket, pushes three fifty-dollar notes into my hand. 'That's for all your hard work so far. But remember what I said, right?'

'About what?'

He smiles, crushes his cigarette butt out on the floor.

'Good answer.'

•

The utility pants feel much better and cleaner than the jeans. I put on a black polo neck t-shirt, then check myself out in the bathroom mirror. My skin has already started to darken from being outside every day. I comb my hair with my fingers.

A permanent job. It could really change things.

It'd be great to get my own place, then maybe invite her down. But even if she didn't want to come, at least I'd be secure.

If I end up back on the street, I'll be back inside soon enough. I've seen it happen too many times. Blokes got released and couldn't get stable accommodation. Whatever they earned inside would be gone pretty soon. The friends they used to have didn't want to know them, their family burnt too many times.

In the end, the only people who'd accept them were other crooks. Before long, they'd breach their parole or reoffend. Either way, they'd be back inside.

Could I really have been wrong about how deep the grave was?

I know what I saw.

I grab my jacket, head out of the shed and through the north gate.

I walk along Macpherson Street, on the footpath on the opposite side to the cemetery. It's Victorian terraces, mostly. The people mustn't be bothered by living near a cemetery. Maybe it makes you appreciate what you've got, while you've still got it. I pass an old Anglican church. I wonder if people still go there, and if there's really any point.

I turn right onto Lygon Street, walk down the footpath on the cemetery side. It's a shared path with bicycles, and a few hurtle past in the opposite direction, travelling north. Students and office workers and the like, probably heading home for the day.

Cyril had knocked off early, to my relief. I didn't fancy the idea of telling him about the journo, but maybe he already knows. Krystal might've told him. Either way, I don't want to bring it up. I don't want anything to ruin my chances at the job.

I cross the road, walk along the eastern side of Lygon Street. I go past a double-storey building with arched windows and 'Eolian Hall' painted in bold black letters above the door. I wonder what it means. I spot Filou's on the corner up ahead, a small cafe with a few tables scattered on the footpath. I realise it's the same place as where Cyril gets the pies.

Neville is seated on the Fenwick Street side. He's got a lit cigarette dangling from his mouth, a broadsheet newspaper spread out in front of him. He folds up the paper when he sees me, butts out his cigarette.

'Here he is, the man of the moment. So, what can I get you? A bit of cake, coffee? The vanilla slice is worth crossing town for, so I'm told.'

I sit down.

'Just a coffee. Cappuccino.'

He smiles. 'Old school. Back in a jiff.'

I pick up the newspaper. It's a copy of *The Argus*, folded to the opinion and letters page. Neville returns with a tall bottle of water and a couple of glasses. He's still limping slightly.

'What's wrong with your leg?'

He shakes his head. 'Got bitten by a shark.'

'Seriously?'

'Nah, just yanking your chain. Not such an exciting story, sadly. Always been like this, ever since birth. One's a bit shorter than the other, you see.'

He fills my glass.

'Does it give you trouble?'

He shrugs. 'I'm supposed to wear a shoe lift, but I can't be arsed. It's not like I need to be running marathons. Enjoying the read?'

I put the newspaper down. 'I didn't really start.'

He nods. 'Not many read the print version these days, which is a shame. People used to get exposed to a lot of different perspectives, read topics outside of their comfort zone. Most people get their news online now, which means they get pulled in by clickbait or just stay in their silos. It's not good for society. Might be the beginning of the end.'

'Clickbait?'

'Ah, don't get me started. Anyway, I appreciate you coming.'

I take a sip of my water. It's warm.

'No worries. But I was wondering about something. How did you find me? I mean, how did you know I was staying at the hostel?'

He links his hands behind his head, leans back in his chair.

'I've got a few contacts here and there. Some friends in low places, you might say. When you've been around as long as me, they tend to accumulate. As do the favours owed. Bottom line is, I know a bloke at Corrections who tells me about the high-profile releases, where they're headed. It can be pretty newsworthy. Say it's some paedophile, for example. I can see if they're gonna live near a school or the like. It's not the sort of stuff I like to write, a bit sensationalist, but useful if I'm desperate.

'In your case, he gave me the hostel address. Apparently you'd told one of the social workers where you were headed, but I knew there was no guarantee you'd still be there. More importantly, he told me you'd changed your name a while back. A few pull that trick, especially now that pretty much everything is on the web. Is that why you did it?'

I shake my head. 'I just wanted a clean break. To leave the past behind, you know? To start with a clean slate.'

The waitress arrives with two coffees, a slice of chocolate cake.

'Thanks, love,' he says. 'The cake's for me.'

I have a sip of my coffee. It's good.

'Why me, though?' I say. 'I'm not exactly high-profile. I mean, I know it got a bit of press when we got sentenced, but it was a long time ago.'

He swallows a spoonful of cake.

'Mate, you shouldn't underestimate yourself. I don't think you realise how much attention your case got, especially when it went to court. "The Vigilante Killers" – that's what we called you. Every crime story needs a good catchphrase, I reckon. Anyway, it was all over the news. Not just newspapers, though. TV, radio, the works. I mean, the story had everything.

'People love these small-town crime yarns. And the community was really divided about what you did, which sells newspapers.

Some thought you were a hero, others thought they should throw away the key. It's the kind of story that writes itself. I was a court reporter back then, still pretty green. But you got me my first front page. I've never forgotten about it. Wasn't my best work, but still.'

'I'm happy for you.'

He smiles. 'I can handle the sarcasm. Look, I'm pretty used to people being unhappy to see me. I'm usually there on the worst day of their life, or near to it. I mostly do features now. Which is where you come in. My editor is keen for me to write about your release. Especially since you're working at the cemetery. I mean, the irony of it is bloody spectacular. He came from one of the tabloids, so he's pushing the paper in a new direction. But I want to take a slightly different tack, give you a chance to tell your story.'

'Sounds like you already know it.'

He frowns. 'I don't mean the crime, so much. I'm talking about your return to the community. I know it's tough when you get released, especially if you don't have many supports.'

I finish my coffee, pour myself another water.

'Bottom line is, I'd rather not do the scandal-sheet crap my editor wants. I'd rather give it a more human angle, talk about the challenges of rebuilding your life. Get some of the charities and post-release organisations to comment, that type of thing. We'd have to touch on what happened, of course, but it wouldn't be the focus.'

'And if I don't want to talk?'

He shakes his head. 'Then I won't have much to work with. So it'll likely be something sensationalist. And I don't reckon the cemetery would be too happy with that kinda press. I have my ethics, but I also need to pay the bills. I've got kids, you know.'

I look out to the road and the cemetery beyond. 'I'd rather just put it behind me. It was years ago. I want to move on with my life.'

He takes a cigarette out of a pack in his shirt pocket, lights it.

'Look, I'll be blunt. This article is gonna be written one way or another. But the type of story I want to write could be a good thing for you.'

'How so?'

'Well, you'd get to tell your story the way *you* want to. Who knows, some of the TV current affairs shows might follow up on it, might want an interview.'

He takes a deep drag.

'Think about it. It'll be your chance to set the story straight. And that bird you're chasing up in Queensland? She might think you're a bit of a star.'

I shake my head. 'You're really clutching at straws now.'

He smiles, takes another drag.

'Look, you don't have to give me an answer right now. Why don't you mull it over. I'll come see you in a couple of days, see how you feel about it then.'

He stands up, dusts the crumbs from his pants.

'I'd better get moving, though. The traffic through the city at this time of day is a killer, and I have to pick up the kids from some after-school crap. It never ends.' He takes one last drag of his cigarette, then shakes my hand. 'Thanks again for coming.'

'Sure. By the way, can I ask a favour?'

'Name it.'

'That contact you've got at Corrections, can you find something out for me?'

He nods.

'A prisoner named Ali Tabak. Ali the Turk, they called him. Just wondering where he ended up.'

'Friend of yours?'

'Not exactly. We shared a cell.'

'No worries.'

He picks up the newspaper, folds it under his arm.

'Oh, there was one last thing I meant to ask. Why'd you go with "Tom"? I mean, you could've picked any name at all.'

I shrug. 'Didn't think about it too much.'

He smiles. 'Clearly. But for what it's worth, I think Fab suits you better.'

'UTTER SAVAGERY': VIGILANTE KILLERS SENTENCED

By Neville Barton

A Supreme Court judge has described the murder and mutilation of a notorious paedophile as 'horrific', as he sentenced two men for the crime.

Ben Carver, 29, was jailed for a maximum of seven years for the 1995 murder of Ronald Bellamy. His accomplice, Fabrizio Morressi, also 29, was sentenced to a maximum of nine years imprisonment. Both men had pleaded guilty.

It was a packed courtroom that witnessed the sentencing, with gasps heard from the public gallery as the sentences were handed down.

The court heard that Mr Carver was 18 years old when he murdered Mr Bellamy, attacking him with a rock at an isolated property near Stawell, in western Victoria. Mr Morressi witnessed the crime, then dismembered and disposed of Mr Bellamy's body in an act described by the judge as 'utter savagery'. Mr Bellamy's remains were not discovered until eleven years later, concealed inside a wheelie bin and dumped in the Wimmera River.

The court also heard that Mr Bellamy had a 'significant history' of child sex offending, and it was alleged that he had sexually abused Mr Carver. Mr Carver's barrister, Violetta Rosetti, argued that Mr Bellamy's alleged offending mitigated Mr Carver's culpability. She said that while he had tried hard to overcome the alleged abuse, it had 'a lasting and pervasive impact.' She also said Mr Carver's crime was spontaneous, motivated by vengeance alone.

In sentencing Mr Carver, Justice John Pemmick said, '[T]he community holds the violation of children, especially sexually, as among the most vile and despised acts.' While he had sympathy for Mr Carver's situation, he was 'concerned that anything less than a severe sentence may be viewed as a lessening of culpability for crimes such as his.'

In sentencing his accomplice, Mr Morressi, Justice Pemmick described his actions as 'the most serious violation of a corpse I have come across in twenty-three years.' He said that he 'went to great lengths to conceal the crime and demonstrated a high degree of forethought.'

While Justice Pemmick accepted the alleged sexual abuse of Mr Carver was a mitigating factor in his defence, it was not sufficient to warrant a reduction in Mr Morressi's sentence, stating that he is 'capable, if not likely, to commit serious crimes in the future.'

Ms Rosetti said Mr Morressi accepted his crimes were serious, but argued his actions were motivated by 'a misplaced and misdirected loyalty for his childhood friend.'

Outside the court, Detective Inspector Roy MacGee praised the work of Homicide Squad detectives in bringing the offenders to justice.

'Our officers were tireless in their effort to solve this terrible crime. Given the passage of time it was an especially complex and challenging investigation, and it is a credit to each of our members that we can finally bring this matter to a close.'

Mr Carver will be eligible for parole in 2010, while Mr Morressi will be eligible for parole in 2012.

Part Three

One

I drop my coins into the slot and dial the number. It rings three times.

'Hello?'

'It's me.'

'I haven't got long.'

'You've never got long.'

'You need to be more careful.'

'What do you mean?'

She sighs. 'Derek's had a few calls where the caller hung up as soon as he answers. I wonder who that could be?'

'I didn't know the best time.'

'There is no best time. Anyway, how have you been?'

'Good. The job's going well. They've made me full-time.'

'That's great, Tom.'

'Yeah. It's better money, so I'll be able to . . . anyway, it's much better.'

'I'm glad it's going well.'

'Listen, did some journo call you?'

'Yeah, I was gonna tell you about that. A little while back, not long after we spoke. Said he got my number from someone at the prison. He knew you'd been calling me.'

'We have to give them our list of contacts. The prison, I mean.'

'Anyway, it was lucky I got the call. If Derek—'

'I don't want to cause any trouble.'

'It's a bit late for that. So, did you talk to him? He didn't really explain what it was about.'

'He reported on my case way back when. He's just curious about what I'm up to, now I'm out.'

'Really? It was a long time ago.'

'Yeah, I'm sure it'll go away. So, listen, remember how I said about maybe coming up there? Well, I've been thinking. I'll get some time off in July, so I could come up for a few days around then, if that works. I'd stay in a caravan park or something, so there'd be no pressure. We could just have a coffee.'

'I . . . I dunno.'

'I won't cause you any hassles. I know you're with Derek and—'

She sighs. 'We're just . . . we've been going through a bit of a rough patch lately. I don't want to risk things.'

'I'm sorry to hear that.'

'Yeah, I'm sure you are. Of course I'd like to see you, but I just need to be careful. It feels too risky.'

'Risky like that time in the pantry? When Bob was asleep upstairs?'

She laughs. 'Now, that really *was* risky.'

I can hear the smile in her voice. It makes me smile too.

'I'd love to see you.'

The receiver is hot against my ear.

'I know, but let's just leave it for now.'

'When can I call you again?'

'Next week?'

'Wednesday?'

'Three o'clock. No later, though.'

'Okay.'

'And no more hang-up calls.'

'Yep. I promise.'

•

Before I go back to the shed, I head to the office. I push open the heavy wooden door, step inside. The air is musty and cool. Krystal is standing behind the counter, sealing a tall stack of envelopes.

'Hello, stranger. You're looking chipper.'

'Yeah?'

I try not to smile, to hold it in.

'A bit happier than normal, that's for sure. Which probably isn't saying much. Anyway, I guess congratulations are in order.'

'What for?'

'For getting the job, of course. Welcome aboard and all that. But I'm guessing this isn't a social visit. You come to get your pay?'

'Is now a good time?'

'Sure.'

She clips out back in her heels, returns after a minute or two with a yellow envelope.

'You'll need to get your bank account sorted, though. I can't keep paying you cash.'

'Will do.'

'It's good you stopped by, actually. Can you let the boys know we've got a burial this Thursday? Tell Cyril I'll give him the details later.'

'Righto.'

'By the way, did you end up talking to that journo? I tried to fend him off, but he's a tenacious little bugger.'

'Yeah. It was nothing, though.'

She arches an eyebrow. 'You could've fooled me. What was it about?'

'He didn't say?'

'Just said you were an old acquaintance.'

'About right.'

She frowns. 'Was it about what you did?'

Neville must've told her.

'What do you mean?'

'Cyril told me the story. How you got caught up in helping a mate. You went to jail for it? Is that right?'

'Pretty much.'

She rolls her eyes. 'Fair dinkum, it's like getting blood from a stone with you. Have you always been like this?'

I shrug. 'I just don't like talking about it. It's like I was a different person back then.'

She sighs. 'I know that feeling. But the past has got this funny way of following us around. You're not exactly Robinson Crusoe in that respect. Everyone's got a history, a few skeletons in the closet. Take Stitch, for example.'

'Stitch?'

'Yeah, that's Cyril's nickname from years ago. But you'd know about that, wouldn't you?' There's a smile at the edge of her lips. 'I mean, seeing how you and him go way back.'

My eye starts to twitch. I hope she doesn't notice.

'I've never heard anyone call him that. And he's never told me much about his past.'

'Now, that's a surprise. Normally you can barely shut that bloke up. But you know he used to be mixed up with the bikies, right?'

'Not sure he ever mentioned it. Or maybe he did and I forgot.'

She shrugs. 'Look, it's probably not something he likes to advertise. He was never fully patched or anything. He was a bit of a gun saddle-maker, once upon a time, but he lost his job when the company moved offshore. He had a couple of mates in the Bandidos, so they gave him some work.'

'Doing what?'

'Their jackets and such, if you can believe it. Which is why they called him "Stitch". Real imaginative. You sure he never told you?'

'Not that I remember.'

'Anyway, he got caught up in some pretty heavy stuff.'

'Really?'

She nods. 'It's probably not my story to tell. I just meant that everyone's got something in their past.'

'You too?'

She smiles. 'So, what you gonna do with all that cash?'

'Save it.'

'That doesn't sound like much fun.' She taps her nails on the counter, the diamond ring sparkles. 'You should treat yourself.'

I shrug. 'Maybe.'

'Well, up to you. But either way, it's good to have you on board. And don't forget to tell Cyril to come see me about that burial. It'll be over near the shed, not far from the north gate, so nice and convenient.'

'Will do.'

As soon as I get out of the office, I open the envelope. There are five fifty-dollar notes, a crisp hundred, and a couple of twenties. Almost four hundred dollars, all told.

I try not to smile, but I can't help it.

•

It's been a long time since I've been in a supermarket. This one feels different than any I remember. It's cold inside, too cold, the decor a throwback to the 1970s. Timber veneer panelling and terrazzo tile floors. Classic hits over a tinny sound system.

It was Cyril who recommended the place.

'You could go to Safeway or Coles, but I hate those bastards. Greedy corporations who screw everyone. Their suppliers, employees, the customers too. Piedimonte's is the way to go, over in North Fitzroy. A bit more expensive, but they have better stuff.'

It was a decent walk to get there, but it felt good. The money in my pocket and the phone call with Lucy. I'm trying hard to keep my happiness in check, just in case I jinx it.

It feels strange to be among the shoppers, just ordinary people going about their day. Parents with noisy schoolkids, old ladies and their canvas trolleys. It makes me feel part of something. Something normal and ordinary. Good and real.

I get a few cans of baked beans, a ciabatta loaf, some prosciutto from the deli. The prosciutto was more expensive than I expected. I pick up a couple of pre-made meals as a treat.

A middle-aged lady is working the register, her hair wrapped up in a net. She looks Italian, but I'm not completely sure.

'Prosciutto, ah?' she says. 'San Daniele too. Always the best one.'

'Good to know. How's your day been?'

'It's good, good.'

'I used to work in a supermarket myself. Years ago.'

She shrugs. 'It's okay here. I just live around the corner, so it suits me.'

'I didn't work the checkout, just collecting trolleys.'

'When you were a kid?'

The hot carpark in summer. Dion breathing down my neck. Afriki, the Sudanese kid with the big smile.

I shrug. 'Sort of.'

'Where you work now?'

'I'm a gardener.'

'Ah, it's good to work outside, in nature.' She rings up the total. 'That's thirty-three dollars and fifty cents.'

I reach into my pocket, take out the envelope.

'Pay day, ah? It go quick nowadays, especially in this place.'

Outside the supermarket, I spot a couple of dogs tied to a pole. Two greyhounds, one black and the other grey, both in matching striped jackets. I stop and give the black one a pat. He eyes me cautiously.

It'd be great to get a dog, maybe once I get my own place and get settled.

Further along the footpath, a beggar sits cross-legged with a hat beside him. There's a handwritten cardboard sign leaning up against the wall. I don't read it. I drop a few coins into his hat.

'Thanks, brother,' he says.

•

It's the best dinner I've had in as long as I can remember. Beef stroganoff with rice, washed down with three cans of beer. It's dark by the time I finish, but I don't feel tired enough for bed.

I head straight through the middle of the cemetery this time, via North Avenue. There's a cool and gentle south-westerly, and all is quiet. Suddenly, I hear wings flapping above. I look up. A tawny frogmouth, or maybe a fruit bat, silhouetted against the slate-grey sky.

Once I get to the bluestone chapel, I turn right and take Seventh Avenue back toward the shed. I keep an eye out, but don't see a fox this time. During the day, I'd taken care to look for any dens. I figure they might be living under the old broken monuments, beneath the cracked ledger stones that lie flat atop the graves. In the cool, dark void where the earth has sunken in.

Further along Seventh Avenue, nearer Macpherson Street, I notice a few more gaps in the fence where the iron posts have come loose. They mustn't have the money to replace them.

The wind picks up through the trees, carries the smell of gum leaves. I close my eyes, feel the air on my skin.

I remember.

A dam outside of town, the height of summer. Ben has brought his nets, but I'm sticking to the handlines. I've got the idea that I get bigger yabbies that way. It never works. Neither of us are catching many, and after a while we retreat to the shade.

We sit with our backs against the gum tree, on opposite sides, talking shit and throwing stones into the dam.

'You gonna play cricket this year?'

'Yeah.'

'Who for?'

'Dunno. What about you?'

'Maybe Great Western.'

'Yeah. I might too then.'

It feels like that day, that summer, might never end. Time stretches out ahead of us, filled with bright hope and promise. No hints of a damaged future.

I open my eyes, catch movement in my peripheral vision. I look around, but there's nothing there. I close my eyes.

Another memory.

A winding, narrow back road, the pitch black of night. Bright headlights pierce the tree line as we round each bend. The heavy weight in the boot bounces with each pothole and corrugation.

Neither of us speak.

It flashes across the road in front of the car, its long bushy tail lit up by the headlights. I must've only missed it by a split second. It disappears into the undergrowth, the darkness.

I turn to look at Ben.

His silhouette, his silence.

If I'd known then what I know now, what would I have done? Would I have gone to the police and turned him in? Could I have let him take the fall?

Footsteps behind me now, crunching leaves.

My heart beats hard in my chest.

I turn around.

There's no-one.

This place is starting to get to me. The sooner I can get enough money, get out of here and into my own place, the better.

I reach into my pocket, give my lucky charm a squeeze.

I head up the road and back toward the shed.

Two

The next day starts with weeding on the west side of the cemetery, not far from the newest mausoleum. I dig out the bigger weeds with a spade, while Seamus sprays Round-Up.

'Don't know why you bother with the spade,' he says. 'Much easier this way.'

'Yeah, great for the environment too.'

I hear slow footsteps coming down the path behind me.

I stop weeding, turn around.

'Krystal said I'd find you up this way.'

It's the journo.

Seamus stops spraying, looks him up and down.

'Seamus, this is Neville,' I say.

Seamus nods.

'Good to meet you, Seamus. You're Irish, I'm guessing?'

Seamus doesn't answer, goes back to his spraying.

'Similarly loquacious.'

Seamus turns, narrows his eyes.

'What's that sposed to mean?'

Neville shakes his head. 'Never mind. So, Tom, have you got time for that chat?'

I pick up my spade. 'I've got a lot of work to get done.'

'I've already cleared it with management, if that's what you're worried about. She's happy for you to take a break. We can grab a coffee over the road.'

I shake my head. 'We've got a grave to get ready this arvo. So maybe some other time.'

Seamus stops his spraying. 'I can finish up here, Tom. I mean, if you need to split for a bit.'

'You sure?'

He nods. 'The longer we take here, the more Cyril will have done on that grave, and the less for us to do. I'll meet you at the gravesite after.'

I take a deep breath in and out, lean my spade against a headstone. Maybe it's best to just get it over with.

Neville smiles.

'This won't take long, I promise.'

•

Two of the three outside tables are taken at Filou's. There are retirees on one, some Lycra-clad cyclists on the other. Three expensive-looking Italian bikes are leaning against the wall.

We sit on the Lygon Street side. It's noisier there, with the traffic and trams rushing past.

'First things first,' Neville says. 'Your mate, Ali Tabak.'

'He isn't my mate.'

He shrugs. 'I asked my source at Corrections to do a bit of digging. Seems he got moved to Fulham Prison about six months before the end of his sentence.'

'Does he know where he went? Once he got out?'

'Yeah, he knows exactly where. The cemetery at Fawkner. Got on the wrong end of a shiv just a few days shy of his release.'

'He got stabbed?'

He nods. 'They took him to hospital but he was dead on arrival. Must've rubbed someone up the wrong way.'

I feel a wave of relief wash through me.

'You don't seem too cut up about it,' he says. 'If you'll excuse the pun.'

I fill my water glass. 'I guess not.'

'Anyway, down to business. Are you happy for me to record this?'

Neville doesn't wait for an answer. He places his mobile phone on the table between us, presses a red button on its screen.

I take a sip of my coffee. It's not as good as the last time.

'So, I want to start way back, if we could. Just some back-ground info. I want to take you back to when you were kids. You and Ben, back in Stawell.'

I look out at the passing traffic, then across the road to the cemetery. I wonder how much Cyril might have done on his own by now. How much will be left for me and Seamus.

'Did you hear me?'

'I heard.'

'Do you remember when Ronnie Bellamy came to town?'

After Daisy, Ben's neighbour from up the street, killed herself.

I nod. 'Yeah.'

'If I remember correctly from the court case, he moved in just a few doors from Ben. Is that right?'

'Yeah, that's right.'

'And Ben was helping him out, doing chores for some pocket money?'

Not just chores, though.

'Yep.'

'Can you tell me when you first thought something might have been amiss. I mean, about the relationship between Bellamy and Ben?'

The porno magazine. The new runners Ronnie paid for. The time I saw Ben getting into Ronnie's car out the front of school.

I shake my head.

'I can't remember. Not exactly.'

'Is there anything that sticks in your mind about Bellamy? Anything unusual.'

The blue Statesman De Ville. His eyes, the way one seemed a different colour than the other. The thick green veins mapping his arms.

'I'm not sure I can talk about this.'

'I just need it for some context. It won't be the focus.'

I shake my head. 'I'd rather not.'

'Okay, let's fast-forward a bit then. We can backtrack later, if you feel up to it. So, how about we start from the court case. What did it feel like when you heard the judge handing down the sentence?'

'Mine or Ben's?'

'Yours. Or both, if you like.'

His empty gaze, staring out into the courtroom. He'd already decided.

I swallow.

'It was a long time ago.'

'Well, just try to take yourself back to it. To the courtroom, I mean. If I remember correctly, Ben got sentenced first, then you. Is that right?'

'Yeah.'

'What did it feel like hearing his sentence? What was going through your mind?'

I pick up my coffee, but my hand starts to shake. I put the cup back down. I look out to the road again, watch as a truck thunders past. My lip starts to tremble. I try to stop it, but I can't.

He reaches across the table, stops the recording.

'Fuck, mate. Are you alright?'

I nod. 'Yeah.'

'We can take a breather if you like. Hang on a sec, I'll get you something.'

Neville disappears inside for a minute, then returns with a thick wad of serviettes.

'Best I could do.'

'Thanks.'

'Are you okay to keep going?'

I nod.

Neville reaches across the table, turns the recording back on.

'Things were . . . when we were kids, things were different. We just didn't know. But I . . . I thought something might be wrong, you know? I had a feeling. But I couldn't find the words. And even if I could, there was no-one I could tell.'

'What did you notice about Ronnie?'

I shake my head. 'He was just . . . it was a feeling, more than anything. He made me uncomfortable. He scared me. There was something weird about him, the way he acted. Like it was all for show, like it wasn't real. Like what he said didn't really match up with what he was thinking. But it was mostly little things that didn't add up. I started to get the feeling something was wrong.'

'With Ben?'

I nod. 'Yeah.'

'What did you notice about him? Had something changed?'

He didn't want to be my friend. He blamed me for what was happening.

I take a deep, ragged breath.

'I'm sorry, I don't think I can do this. I thought I could, but it's too hard.' I wipe my cheeks. 'He was my best mate, you know? He always looked out for me.'

'It's okay.' Neville reaches over to his phone, turns off the recording. 'Look, for what it's worth, I've got no issue with what you boys did. As far as I'm concerned, you and Ben did the world a favour. You should've been given a medal, if anything.'

I shake my head. 'I just wish things could've been different. I wish I could've told someone what was happening.'

Neville puts his phone back in his pocket.

'I've got boys of my own, you know. Times have changed, but it scares me to think there's still people like that around. They're manipulators. And even if they get caught, the justice system can't fix things. They go to jail, do the programs, then get back out and do the same thing again. You would've seen it yourself.'

I take a deep breath in and out.

'I'm just trying . . . I want to put that all behind me, you know? I want to make something of myself, to have a normal life. So it doesn't seem like it was all for nothing. I've got this job now and . . . I just want a fresh start.'

Neville finishes the last of his coffee, lets out a long sigh.

'Look,' he says, 'I'll tell you what. I'll have a chat to my editor, try to talk him around. Maybe there's no story here after all.'

'You could do that?'

He nods. 'I can't make any promises, but just leave it with me. I've got some other ideas I can pitch. But in the meantime, you better get back to work. That grave won't dig itself.'

He heads inside, pays for our coffees. When he comes back out, he lights a cigarette.

'I'll be in touch, okay? I'll let you know how I go with the boss.'

'Yep. Thanks.'

'One last thing I meant to ask, just out of curiosity. How long have you known Cyril?'

'Why?'

He takes a drag of his cigarette. 'Oh, it's just that Krystal mentioned you were old mates. Did you meet inside?'

I shake my head.

'Ah, no worries. Just thought I'd check.'

•

On the way back to the cemetery, light rain begins to fall. I head toward the north gate, spot the Wacker just a few rows up from the Chinese section.

There's no sign of Seamus or Cyril.

I head back to the shed. The roller door is up and I see Cyril is inside, sitting on the bench. Lina is asleep at his feet.

'Welcome back,' he says.

Lina wakes, runs up and jumps on my leg. I give her a scratch behind her ear.

'How come you're not digging?'

He lights a cigarette, exhales a thin stream of smoke.

'You didn't notice the wet stuff falling from the sky? Sometimes you've gotta get it done in the rain, but it's better if we can wait it out. If she fills with water, we've gotta pump it clean before the burial. Pain in the arse, and I could do without the stress.'

'Where's Seamus?'

'Making the most of the rain interval to get us some beers for later.' He gives me a look. 'Are you alright?'

'Yeah, fine.'

'You don't look fine.'

I shrug.

'Why don't you pull up a pew?'

I sit down beside him on the bench. Lina leans her weight on my leg. The smell of Cyril's cigarette is making me queasy.

'So, what's up?'

'Nothing.'

'You sure about that?'

'Yeah.'

'How'd it go with the journo? Neville, isn't it? Seamus told me he came to see you again.'

I shrug.

'Jesus, mate. You must've been great company for your cellmates over the years. The time must've just flown.'

He takes another drag of his cigarette.

'What's he want to write about? I'm guessing it's about how you chopped up that pedo into little bits. Am I right?'

I grip the edge of the bench.

'How do you know about that?'

He smiles. 'Krystal squeezed it out of him. He told her that he wrote about your case way back when. As it turns out, it seems we have a bit in common, me and you.'

'Like what?'

He takes another drag, flicks the butt out through the roller door. 'I'll fill you in some other time. For what it's worth, I think it pretty much makes you a hero. Blokes like that don't deserve to walk among us.'

'I'm not sure about that. The hero bit, I mean.'

'You want to talk about it?'

'Nah.'

'Jeez, that's a surprise. So, did you tell the journo to rack off?'

'Sort of.'

He gives me a nudge. 'Look, how about I have a chat to Krystal. We can make sure that bloke leaves you alone from now on. We look after our own here, you know.'

He stands up, steps outside the roller door, looks up to the sky.

'It should start to clear fairly soon, I reckon. Then we can get back into it.' He sits back down on the bench. 'Hopefully we can get it all done before dusk.'

'Who's getting buried?'

He shrugs. 'Some young bloke in his twenties. Suicide, apparently. He stepped out on the train tracks, just on the other side of a bend in Parkville. Did it so the driver wouldn't have time to stop. Pretty common manoeuvre, so I'm told.'

Ben in his jail cell, the torn bedsheet.

I push the thought away.

'Bloody sad for the family. The poor train driver too. But you know, there's some philosophers who reckon it's the only rational thing to do. Suicide, I mean. Because life has no meaning, at least in their view.'

'Sounds pretty extreme.'

He nods. 'Not sure I agree with them, either. Anyway, it could take us a while to dig this one. It's an awkward spot, between a couple of big monuments.'

'Just a single, isn't it?'

'Yeah, it is meant to be a single.' He leans down, gives Lina a pat. 'But we might go a bit deeper.'

'Deeper?'

He sits back, crosses his arms. He stares out through the roller door.

'Listen, I'm gonna fill you in on something. But I need to know you'll keep it to yourself.'

'Who am I gonna tell?'

'Maybe that bird you're chatting to? Or the journo?'

'Nah.'

'All the same. I need your word.'

I shake my head. 'I won't say anything.'

He nods. 'Seamus won't be happy with me, but I trust my instincts. There's only a few of us in the loop, and it has to stay that way.'

'What's this about?'

He reaches down again, gives Lina a scratch behind her ear.

'Well, from time to time we dig the single graves a little deeper. Because sometimes, we need to accommodate someone extra.'

My throat goes tight. 'What do you mean?'

'The results of a professional hit, you might say. Gangland stuff. You get me?'

I swallow.

'So it wasn't my imagination, was it? The other grave?'

He nods. 'Look, it can be pretty hard to get rid of a body these days, especially in the city. Cameras all over the place, on the roads and everywhere. Even parts of this cemetery, as you know.'

'So you—'

'For the right price, of course. And, like I say, it's only every now and again. It's great money for not much work. And you'll get a healthy cut.'

My breath catches in my throat.

'I . . . I don't know. I don't want to end up back inside.'

'Mate, the only way that'll happen is if you talk. And that's not in your interest, whichever way you slice it.'

'Who are they, though? The ones getting buried?'

He crosses his arms.

'We're not talking decent law-abiding folk, here. These are people mixed up in some pretty bad shit. Drug trafficking, mostly. They live by the sword, die by the sword. Bottom line is, there aren't too many people who are gonna miss them. And sometimes it's better for everyone if it seems like they've just disappeared. Like they shot through interstate, or whatever.'

'I dunno.'

'I'm talking serious cash here. You could get yourself a real nice place, impress that bird. Get yourself a car, maybe. Take her on a trip somewhere.'

'Why me, though? I mean, can't you and Seamus do it?'

He shakes his head. 'Like I've told you, digging a grave is a two-man job. And that bloke is getting less and less reliable.'

'And if I say no?'

He smiles, takes out his pack, lights another cigarette.

'Something tells me you won't.'

I hear footsteps approaching. Seamus steps in through the roller door, carrying a six-pack of beers. He gives Cyril a look.

'Looks like I'm interrupting something.'

Cyril grins. 'Take a guess.'

Seamus shakes his head. 'You're sure this is a good idea?'

'Absolutely.' He slaps me on the back. 'He's already on board.'

•

It's almost dark by the time we get it done.

It was a slow and difficult dig, like Cyril said. The surrounding graves made it hard to get the Wacker close enough, the angles too acute.

'Bitch of a job,' Cyril says. 'We'll clean her up in the morning, I reckon. Just grab that sheet of plywood and cover her up for now.'

Me and Seamus lift the plywood and place it over the grave. Cyril shifts the bricks on top, then the witches hats in each corner.

'Job's right,' Seamus says. 'Beer o'clock?'

Cyril shakes his head.

'Not for me. This took a bit longer than I expected. I need to get Lina home, then I've got trivia. We're out for revenge tonight. But I'll see you blokes bright and early tomorrow.'

We tidy up the tools, then head back to the shed. Seamus gets two beers from the fridge, joins me on the bench.

'Cheers,' he says. He takes a deep drink. 'That was a real fucker. At least we got it done before dark, though.'

The young man being buried. The suicide. I wonder how his family would feel if they knew there was another body beneath.

I scull my beer, try to push the thought away.

'How long has this been going on?'

He shrugs. 'At least as long as I've been here. Maybe five years or so? Maybe longer. I dunno how long they were doing it before, Cyril and Kev. Never asked. I figure it's better not to know.'

I take another drink.

'You having second thoughts?'

'Nah.'

'It's a bit late for cold feet, you know? You're already in it.'

'I just . . . I feel bad for the kid's family. The one getting buried tomorrow. The suicide.'

He shakes his head. 'You gotta remember that half this cemetery is probably recycled graves, but we just don't know about them. They got up to all sorts of shit back in the old days.'

'Still, it doesn't make it right. Does it?'

'You think it makes any difference to the dead bloke?'

'Which one?'

'Either.'

'It's just . . . well, what if we get caught?'

He shakes his head.

'The only way we'll get caught is if someone talks. You gotta remember the burial rights here are in perpetuity. Forever. So it's not like anyone will ever uncover what's down there.'

The beer tastes bitter, but I force it down.

'What about Kev?'

'What about him?'

'Was it part of the reason he left?'

His eyes darken. 'I already told you, didn't I? He left because of that girl he was seeing.'

He takes a last swig of his beer, crushes the can.

'Listen, this is a good deal. It runs smooth as shit, there's never any problems. And Cyril's always got your back, you know? He'll always look out for you.'

I shake my head. 'I just don't want to get in any trouble. I don't want to go back inside.'

He sighs. 'Look, I get it. I felt much the same when I first found out. But that bloke has really helped me through some tough times.'

He stares straight ahead, takes a breath in and out.

'Remember I told you about my girlfriend?'

'The one who died?'

He nods. 'It was an overdose, you know. We were both using, but she was just unlucky. Her family wanted her body back in Ireland, to bury her there. But they couldn't afford to repatriate her. Neither could I, of course. Any spare money I had in those days went up my arm. So Cyril paid for it, and he paid for me to go back for the funeral. I tried to repay him, but he wouldn't take it. People have light and shade, you know?'

I finish my beer.

'So, we're good then?' he says.

I nod. 'Yeah. All good.'

'Glad to hear it. I'll see you in the morning.'

•

I'm not sure what time it is, but I know it must be late.

I open my eyes to the darkness, pull my sleeping bag in close. I can hear the slow creaking of the cemetery gate outside, then a low rumble as a car passes through. I listen to the clink of steel as the gate is closed.

I stay as quiet as I can, steady my breathing. Once I can hear the car heading down the road, I get up off the mattress. I pull on my pants, go slowly to the side door.

I take a breath then open it as quietly as I can. Just an inch or two.

There's a sliver of moonlight through the clouds, and the cemetery is washed in soft blue light. Down Fourteenth Avenue, maybe fifty metres away, I can see the silhouette of the car parked on the grassy verge. Its headlights are turned off. It looks like a sedan, maybe silver or white.

A man gets out of the driver's side. He looks tall, broad-shouldered. He goes to the rear of the car, opens the boot.

Another man gets out of the passenger side. He's shorter, solidly built. He goes purposefully to the gravesite, takes off the witches hats. The other man goes to him, helps him lift off the plywood sheet. They lean it against an adjacent grave then study the hole for a moment.

They go to the rear of the car, one each side, then lean into the boot. They lift something heavy from inside, one at each end.

I hold my breath. It looks like a body wrapped in a tarp or carpet, but it's hard to be sure.

They carry it to the gravesite, manoeuvring carefully between the graves. They stop at the graveside. There's a heavy thump as they drop the body inside.

Each of the men takes a shovel. It takes them maybe five minutes, but they're soon satisfied. They pitch the shovels into the pile of dirt, then lift the plywood back into place. I see the shorter man look around, seemingly back in my direction. I close the door a centimetre or two, but I'm sure I can't be seen from so far away.

The taller man says something indecipherable, then climbs into the driver's seat. He starts the car. The shorter man gets in the passenger side, shuts the door.

The driver slowly turns the car back around, the headlights still turned off. They drive back up the road. I close the door and listen as they pass.

The engine idles roughly just outside the gate. I hold

my breath. Then, the sound of the gate creaking shut. The gentle clink of padlock and chain.

I listen as the car slowly accelerates onto Macpherson Street and out into the night. I take off my pants and go back to bed. I pull the sleeping bag to my chin, turn on my side, but I know I won't sleep again tonight.

I close my eyes and wait for morning.

Three

We work quickly in the morning light. Cyril gives instructions, while me and Seamus clean up around the grave as best we can.

I look down just once into the grave. I wonder who it was, why they ended up there. If they really deserved to end their life like this.

I push the thought away.

'Supposed to start at ten, this one,' Cyril says. 'They'll probably be here any minute.'

Once we're done setting up, Seamus heads back to the shed, leaving me and Cyril to handle the burial. Cyril places two steel rods across the grave.

'What are those for?' I say.

'You'll see.'

I'm wearing my new pants, the utility ones, and a khaki shirt Cyril bought me especially. I dust the dirt from my legs and he looks me up and down.

'Fair dinkum, you almost look respectable. Wait, here they come.'

I look up and see a long silver hearse glide slowly through the cemetery gate. Just a few cars follow.

'These ones are usually pretty small,' he says. 'There's still a stigma, you know. Especially if they're religious. Some of the orthodox faiths won't even let you in the church, which is pretty brutal.'

The hearse slowly navigates a tight corner and turns left down the hill. Three cars follow and park on the grassy verge beside the road.

'Make sure you keep a low profile,' Cyril says. 'I'll be helping the undertaker with the coffin, so you're here just in case of an emergency. In case we need an extra set of hands. But I'll also need you to take those rods out once we lift the coffin. I'll give you the signal.'

He explains how the grave's location, the awkwardness of the stonework around it, will make it tricky to get the coffin down smoothly.

'It'll be pretty hands-on, compared to most,' he says. 'No chance of getting a lowering device in there.'

I listen to what I'm told, but my thoughts are elsewhere. The car last night, the two men, the body. I can still hear the heavy thump as it was dropped inside.

Two undertakers get out of the hearse and approach the gravesite. A tall, balding man wearing rimless glasses, and a younger man in his twenties. Both are wearing black suits with a white logo on the breast.

'Morning, George,' Cyril says.

'Cyril,' the older man replies. 'You good to go?'

'Always. Nice to see you brought the young bloke this time. Matthew, isn't it?'

'That's right,' George says. 'Teaching him the ropes so I can retire one day. Hopefully before I end up here.' He smiles, eyes the gravesite. 'This one's going to be a bit ugly, isn't it?'

Cyril glances toward me. 'Nothing we can't handle.'

'New bloke?' George says. 'What happened to Kev?'

'He shacked up with some bird. This is Tom. He's still a bit green, but a fast learner.'

'Good. We don't want any slip-ups here. As you can imagine, the family are a terrible mess. So the quicker this is over, the better.'

On cue, a middle-aged couple walk slowly down the road. The woman is sobbing, dabbing tissues. A man has his arm around her, a terrible hollowness in his eyes.

Must be the parents.

'Alright,' George says quietly, his face suddenly sombre. 'Let's get this show on the road.'

He walks back up the road to greet the couple, his head lowered. The other mourners have now reluctantly gotten out of their cars and are slowly approaching the gravesite. There's maybe ten people altogether.

Once the mourners are assembled, George and Matthew go to the hearse and open the back. They slide the dark timber coffin onto a shiny steel trolley. A large wreath of dark red roses sits on top.

The mother lets out a terrible groan as her son begins his final journey. The husband slides his arms around her back, under her arms. He takes her weight.

George and Matthew carefully wheel the trolley along the road, then lift it onto the concrete footpath. They approach the gravesite slowly, the path cracked and uneven. Matthew stays by the coffin, while George moves nearer the grave. He nods and gestures for the other mourners to come closer.

I look out through the fence, see a jogger passing. A young woman leading a golden retriever. For a split second, our eyes lock.

'Good morning, everyone, and warmest of welcomes. We are here today to honour the life and say farewell to Christopher Kennedy, who died suddenly on the twelfth of May. My name's George McLure from McLure Funerals, and I've been asked to lead this short graveside service. I'm told that Christopher was loved and admired by all who knew him, and I know the support and kind words you've offered his parents, Jim and Margaret, have been of tremendous comfort during this extremely difficult time.

'In keeping with the family's wishes, this will be a very brief graveside service and farewell. You're then invited to join us back at the funeral home for refreshments, and a chance to share your memories of Christopher, and to offer comfort to one another.

'We will now commit Christopher's body to his final resting place, after which you'll be invited to drop a rose from the wreath atop the coffin, as you say your own farewell.'

George nods, and Matthew presses play on a small, mobile stereo. An instrumental version of Leonard Cohen's 'Hallelujah' begins. I watch as George, Cyril, and Matthew go to the coffin. They're joined by a red-faced, overweight man from the group of mourners. Maybe an uncle. His crumpled shirt half-untucked at the waist.

They each take hold of a handle and lift the coffin from the trolley. They walk slowly to the graveside, wordlessly straddle the grave, then place the coffin onto the steel rods. Cyril and George thread the straps underneath and through the handles of the coffin. On the count of three, they take the weight on the straps and lift the coffin from the rods. Cyril gives me a nod, and I quickly remove the rods from underneath. They begin to slowly lower the coffin into the earth.

I watch the boy's mother, her face frozen in horror, the tears streaming down her cheeks. Her husband continues to hold her, his face a wide-eyed look of disbelief.

Once the coffin is fully lowered, George gestures toward the wreath and invites the mourners to take a rose. Cyril goes to my side, gives me a nudge.

'Good job,' he whispers. 'All without a hitch.'

Once the mourners have finished with the roses, George gives Matthew the signal to cut the music.

'Once again, on behalf of Christopher's family, I'd like to thank you all for joining us today. And a reminder that refreshments will be served back at McLure Funerals, and the family warmly invites you to attend. You're welcome to follow us there, but please keep your headlights on so we don't lose you.'

As the mourners walk slowly back to their cars, George gives Cyril a nod.

'Nice work,' he says. 'I'll see you next time.'

George and Matthew climb into the hearse, then slowly lead the mourners up the road and out of the cemetery. I stand on the curb and watch them pull away.

I close my eyes.

A memory.

A warm summer's day, almost thirty years ago. We're out yabbying, me and Ben. A paddock outside of town. It's a dam Ronnie told Ben about, filled with yabbies.

Before we have a chance to bait the nets, the heat of the day suddenly breaks with a southerly change. The sky darkens over the Grampians, a drop in temperature, then a downpour. We take refuge in Ronnie's blue Statesman. The rain doesn't pass, so Ronnie decides we should head for home.

A strange feeling in the car on the way back to town, a thickness in the air. No-one speaks. The wipers squeak against the windscreen, the side windows fog up.

I remember saying something from the back seat, but I can't remember what.

Ronnie drops me out the front of my house. He opens the boot and dumps my yabby nets on the footpath.

I stay and watch as the deep blue Statesman pulls away. The top of Ben's head is just visible in the passenger seat. There's a terrible, heavy feeling in my chest. A pain in my throat.

I stay and watch until the car goes round the corner.

Until it disappears.

I should've said something.

'Are you alright?' Cyril says.

I open my eyes.

'Yeah.'

'What's up?'

'Nothing. Was just reminded of something.'

He shakes his head, slaps me on the back.

'Yeah, these things are never fun, mate. Anyway, we'll give them five minutes or so to clear the area. The last thing they'll want to see is us shovelling dirt on their beloved son. Seamus will bring the Wacker down in a tick, so maybe you can go get us some pies in the meantime.'

He reaches into his pocket, pulls out a thick wad of fifty-dollar notes. He pushes it into my hand.

'This is for you,' he says. 'There's almost three grand there, so I reckon it's your shout for lunch this time.'

'I . . . are you sure?'

'Sure as shit. But keep it to yourself, right? As far as you know, this grave was built for one. Speaking of, you didn't hear or see anything last night, did you?'

I shake my head. But there's something in the way Cyril looks at me, the hint of a smile on his lips.

The shorter, stocky man. It must've been him.

'Nah, I didn't see a thing.'

'That's the right answer, Tom. Now rack off and get us those pies.'

•

After we fill in the grave, we eat our lunch in silence. The sun is high, and a mild north-easterly is beginning to pick up.

Cyril lights a cigarette, takes a deep drag. He screws up his pie bag, pushes it into his pocket.

'I'll take the Wacker back to the shed, you boys get the rest.'

As Cyril drives the Wacker up the road, me and Seamus gather the tools.

'How'd you go with it?' Seamus says.

'Okay.'

'How was the family?'

'A mess.'

Seamus shakes his head. 'Bad combo, this one. Young kid, plus a suicide. They don't get much worse.'

I nod. 'Good to know.'

'More importantly, did you get your cut?'

'Yep.'

He smiles. 'Not bad, eh?'

'Yeah, I guess.'

He frowns. 'Jesus, mate. Don't get too excited.'

I shrug.

'Christ, you can be a miserable prick sometimes. Has anyone ever told you that?'

I pick up a shovel, balance it on my shoulder. I head up the road toward the shed.

In front of the roller door, Cyril is hosing down the Wacker.

'See?' he smiles. 'That wasn't so bad, was it?'

I nod.

'We'll knock off early today, I reckon. But don't go spending that money all at once.'

I lean my shovel up against the inside wall.

'Do you know anything about how he died?' I say.

He frowns. 'Killed himself on the train tracks. I told you that, didn't I?'

'Nah, I mean the one last night.'

As soon as I say it, I know it's a mistake.

He cuts his eyes at me.

'How the fuck should I know?'

He drops the hose, turns off the tap. He comes in close, grabs hold of my shirt, pushes me hard against the shed wall.

His breath is hot on my face, cigarettes and sweat.

'Listen, we've got a bit of an unwritten policy here. We don't talk about that stuff, even among ourselves. What's done is done, right? So, the sooner you put it out of your mind, the better.'

Seamus walks into the shed, dumps a roll of synthetic turf against the wall. He looks at me, then Cyril.

'Did I miss something?'

Cyril gives him a look. 'Can you believe this prick? He gets all that cash, pretty much for nothing, and suddenly develops a conscience.'

Seamus shakes his head. 'I told you this was a bad idea.'

Cyril rolls up the hose, loops it over the tap.

'Anyway, I'm calling it quits,' he says. 'Got somewhere I need to be.'

•

That night, sleep doesn't come easily.

My thoughts swirl on the boy and his funeral, the body buried beneath. The grieving parents and what they don't know.

Then, a dream.

A dusty backyard somewhere. The sun is hot, and there's a high steel fence all around. At one end, an upturned rubbish bin. Behind it, a black trampoline, tipped on its side.

I look down and see a tennis ball in my right hand. One side is covered with blue electrical tape.

I look up and there's a boy there. He's holding a cricket bat in front of the upturned bin. He's marking his crease.

'Over the fence is six and out,' he says. 'Automatic wicky too.'

I take a few steps back, then run in and bowl.

The boy leans back and cuts the ball into the side fence.

'That's four,' he says.

I go back to bowl again. This time, the boy plays me into the leg side.

'That's two. So I'm on six.'

I bowl once more, and the boy cracks the ball over the off-side fence.

'Six and out,' I say.

The boy smiles.

'I made twelve. Let's see how you go.'

I walk up to him.

He passes me the bat.

I take the handle, but he won't let go.

He looks hard into my eyes.

'Why didn't you help me?'

I shake my head. 'What do you mean?'

'Why didn't you do anything? Why did you let them hurt me?'

I pull on the bat, but he still won't let go.

He starts to cry.

'I'm sorry,' I say. 'I didn't know what to do. I'll try to fix things.'

He shakes his head.

'It's too late now. There's nothing you can do.'

I wake suddenly.

Fast breaths going in and out.

I open my eyes and sit up.

It's still dark inside the shed.

I get up from the mattress, go into the bathroom. I turn on the taps and splash water on my face.

I look at myself in the mirror, deep into my eyes.

I turn off the light.

•

The phone rings four times before she answers.

'Hello?'

'It's me.'

'Jesus Christ, Tom. It's early. I thought I told you—'

'I'm sorry, but it couldn't wait.'

'What is it?'

'Look, I can't tell you everything right now. But I might come up there sooner than planned. Maybe in the next couple of weeks.'

A pause. Too long.

'You said it wouldn't be until around July.'

'Things have changed. I'm not sure I can stay in this job.'

'But you only just started.'

'It's not gonna work out.'

'What's going on?'

'I can't tell you right now.'

'Tom, I . . .'

'I've got some cash, so I'll be right for a while.'

'Are you sure this is a good idea?'

'I'll just stay a few days, that's all. No hassles. Then I'll try to find something else.'

'Another job? That won't be easy.'

'We'll see. If worst comes to worst, I could sell that magazine on the street. I've seen blokes do it here.'

'*The Big Issue?*'

'Yeah.'

'You reckon you're cut out for that?'

'Dunno. But I can't stay here either way.'

'What's going on, Tom? Has something happened?'

We're burying murder victims for cash.

'I can't explain now.'

'Look, I better go.'

'Okay. But listen, I'll call you next week. Wednesday, like I promised. I'll tell you more then.'

She sighs. 'Okay.'
'I miss you, Lucy.'
'I have to go.'
The line goes dead.

Four

There's loud knocking at the side door. I turn on my side, pull the sleeping bag up over my head.

'Hello?'

Knock, knock, knock.

'Is anyone there?'

I sit up, push the sleeping bag away from my body. I pull on my jeans, a t-shirt. I rub my eyes.

Probably just some visitor, looking for a grave.

I open the door, shield my eyes from the sun.

'Jesus Christ, mate. You look like shit.'

It's Neville.

'I didn't sleep much last night. Or the night before.'

'Something on your mind?'

I frown. 'What's that sposed to mean?'

'Bit touchy, are we? Or just not a morning person?'

I shake my head. 'Wasn't expecting company, that's all. It's Sunday, you know.'

He nods. 'Yeah, sorry about that. But I'd rather not deal with Krystal or Cyril this time. And I needed to speak to you fairly urgently.'

'What's going on?'

'Can I come in?'

I move out of the doorway. He follows me inside.

'I like what you've done with the place. Got a real lovely gravedigger, shed-like feel. Could be a new thing.'

'It's just temporary.'

'Anywhere we can sit?'

I gesture toward the bench. 'You want coffee?'

'White, no sugar.'

I go to the kitchen, put the kettle on. I splash some water on my face, dry myself with the tea towel. I wait for the kettle to boil, make the coffees, carry them back.

'Cheers,' he says, and clinks his mug against mine. 'Again, I'm sorry about the surprise visit, but I was actually in the neighbourhood, as it happens. Just dropped the kids off for soccer, down at Princes Park.'

'You don't stay and watch?'

He takes a sip of his coffee.

'Sport's not really my bag. Plus, my son's team is hopeless. Coffee's terrible, by the way.'

'What's this about?'

He takes another sip, sits the mug on the bench.

'I had a chat to my editor about what we discussed. I'm sorry to say it didn't go so well. Basically, he said that if I don't want to write the article the way he wants, he'll find someone who will.'

'So?'

'Well, there's a few young roosters who don't have the same scruples as me, believe it or not. They'll give the guy whatever he wants, or probably worse. And what he wants is tabloid shlock.'

'You're gonna write it then?'

He nods. 'I don't have much choice. Only problem is, he's given me a Monday deadline. Tomorrow that is, not next week. Basically, he's setting me up to fail. But I reckon I can get it done, as long as I throw him a bone or two. My focus will still be on your side of the story, but I'll need some more background. About what happened with Ben and Bellamy. Just a few more questions.'

'And if I don't want to answer?'

'Then you'll have some twenty-something doing a hatchet job. Probably won't even bother to speak to you. But you can bet he'll get a photographer to take some choice pics with a telephoto lens, you digging graves and whatnot. I've seen it all before. So this is the lesser of two evils, let me tell you.'

I take a sip of my coffee.

'Is this the last time we'll have to talk about it?'

'I promise.'

I sigh. 'Righto then. Let's just get it over with.'

He smiles. 'Brilliant. I'll ask the tough questions up front, the stuff the editor really wants, then we can move on. But I'll try to make it as painless as I can. Think of it as like ripping off a bandaid.'

He gets out his phone, places it on the bench, presses the red button.

'Right. So, I wonder if we could go back to when you and Ben were eighteen, when you helped get rid of Ronnie Bellamy's body. I remember from the court case how your lawyer said you were mainly motivated to help your friend. That you didn't have skin in the game, as such.'

'Yeah, that's right.'

'But you didn't want Ben to be caught and then punished, given what he'd gone through with Bellamy.'

'Pretty much.'

'So, at what point did you know what Bellamy had done to him? What did he tell you about the abuse?'

My mind is cast back to that night, the party on the outskirts of town. Walking home together on the dark back roads, the cold wind whistling through the trees. We stop and smoke a joint near the Leviathan dam.

'It was just before he killed him. That same night.'

'You never suspected anything before?'

I grit my teeth.

'I . . . no.'

'Look, I know this is difficult, but did he describe what Bellamy did to him?'

'No.'

'What did he tell you?'

'Not much.'

'Then how did you know what happened?'

Ronnie's shack in the Black Ranges. The rusty tin under his bed. The photos.

'I can't talk about it.'

'Mate, I promise this is the worst of it.'

'I'm sorry, I just can't.'

'It'll get easier from here, but I need an answer.'

'Can you stop the recording?'

He sighs, presses the red button on his phone.

'Look, I know it's painful reliving all this. But if I don't write this story, the bloke who does will be ten times worse.'

'I just want to put it behind me.'

'I get it, but it's not that easy. The horse has bolted. But at least I can paint a sympathetic picture, show the readers how you were just a young man trying to help his mate.'

'You don't understand. I told Ben I'd never talk about it. I promised.'

'Mate, I hate to be blunt, but Ben's dead.'

I shake my head.

'It doesn't matter. I gave him my word.'

He sighs. 'I can't say this is gonna work out well for you. Picture the headline: "Notorious Corpse Mutilator Turns Gravedigger".'

'You're serious?'

'I've seen it too many times. They'll get their pics, ask a few funeral mourners what they think about the new employee, then fill in the rest with a mix of half-truths and straight-out lies. After the story breaks, the tabloid media will be chasing you. Radio shock jocks, the works. They'll eat you alive. You'll lose this job for sure.'

'Can't you just use what you've got?'

He shakes his head. 'It won't be enough. Not for my editor.'

I take a deep breath in and out.

'Maybe there's another story you can write.'

He lets out a sigh. 'Mate, I've already tried that.'

'Nah, it's something else. There's something going on in here. They don't want anyone to know.'

He narrows his eyes. 'What are you on about?'

I lean back against the shed wall, close my eyes.

'This could get me into big trouble.'

'Okay, you've got my attention.' He picks up his phone, turns the recording back on. 'So, what's this about?'

I shake my head. 'There's some bad shit going on here.'

He frowns. 'Like what?'

'Criminal stuff. Organised crime.'

'I'll need a bit more than that.'

I turn to face him.

'They're getting rid of bodies.'

'Yeah, no shit. It's a cemetery, last time I checked. Look, I'm probably a bit thick, but you're going to have to spell this one out for me.'

My hand starts to tremble.

If Cyril finds out, there's no telling what he might do.

'Can you wait a few days before you publish anything?'

'I'll do my best. But first, you'd better tell me what this is about.'

I squeeze my eyes shut.

'They bury bodies illegally. Murder victims, organised hits. Dump them in graves with other bodies.'

I open my eyes.

Neville frowns, shakes his head.

'Is this some kind of joke?'

'No.'

'You're serious?'

I tell him about the two burials, how it's been going on for years.

'And you saw them do it?'

'Yeah, they do it for cash. Thousands. Cyril's the main contact, as far as I know.'

'Do you know who they were? I mean, the ones they buried?'

'Professional hits, that's all he told me. Drug related.'

'Can you tell me which graves?'

'Can't say.'

'Can't or won't?'

'Does it matter?'

He shakes his head. 'Mate, this could be huge. And I'd love to write it. But I think you'll probably have to go to the police first.'

I take a deep breath.

'I'm implicated. If I talk, I'll end up back inside.'

'And if you don't, you'll be an accessory. Again. You'll do more time than if you report it now. Any help you give the police will work in your favour.'

I shake my head.

'Nah, I don't want to get involved. I'll probably just shoot through. Maybe head up north. That's why I need you to hold off on the story for a few days. Maybe longer.'

'You think you can go into hiding?'

'Something like that.'

'Mate, it's not that easy to disappear. Especially nowadays. There's always a trace.'

'I've already decided.'

He lets out a sigh.

'If I write it, I'll have to put some questions to the cemetery. Otherwise, it'll never get past legal. Or my editor.'

'It can't look like it came from me.'

'That might not be possible. Is there anyone else who could know? Just to muddy the waters? To give you some plausible deniability?'

'Seamus? Or maybe Kev?'

'Who's Kev?'

'He used to work here.'

He rubs his cheek, frowns. 'I guess I could drop a few red herrings about the source. But I'll have to have a think. Leave it with me.'

He swallows down the last of his coffee.

'I'd better make a move. The soccer will almost be finished.'

I nod. He picks up his phone, stands up.

'I have to be honest, Tom. I can't make any guarantees about how this will play out. If the cemetery denies it, which they almost definitely will, you'll have to go to the police. It's the only way.'

'Let's just wait and see.'

He sighs. 'Look, I probably shouldn't say this, but I don't think you should go down this road. If there's organised crime involved, they'll likely find you before the police do. Either way, it won't end well.'

'What choice have I got?'

He crosses his arms.

'What if you just keep schtum, look for another job? Then, if your conscience gets the better of you, you can report it anonymously to Crime Stoppers down the track. I can just pretend we never had this conversation.'

I shake my head.

'I want to do the right thing this time, or something close to it. Keeping quiet is what got me into trouble before. I don't want to make the same mistakes again.'

He nods. 'I get it. To be honest, what you've told me isn't a complete surprise, given Cyril's history.'

'You mean the bikies?'

'Bikies?' He frowns, shakes his head. 'You don't know?'

'Know what?'

'I did a couple of checks with a police contact. You didn't hear this from me, but it turns out Cyril murdered a German hitchhiker up north, near Echuca. She'd just turned eighteen, the poor thing. Lina Fischer, her name was.'

'*Lina?*'

'Yeah. Does that name mean something to you?'

I stare at the floor.

'Ah, sort of.'

He nods. 'Anyway, it was years ago. In the eighties.'

'What happened?'

'No-one knows exactly, but she'd been missing for nearly a month by the time she turned up. Her body was dumped in a suitcase on the side of the road. Her own suitcase, as it happened. Chopped up in little pieces, she was. Took them a while to identify her because she was in such a bad state.'

I feel the blood drain from my face.

'Luckily a truckie had spotted Cyril picking her up a few weeks before, which is the only reason he got caught. He got charged with her rape and murder, so God only knows what the poor girl went through. He pled guilty to the murder charge, so got a bit of a discount on his sentence. And they couldn't make a rape charge stick, not without physical evidence.

'There were a few other missing women in the area that the coppers think he might've been involved in, but he covered his tracks pretty well. The story barely got a mention in the news at the time, apparently. The government was worried it would hurt tourism. Suppression orders all over it.

'He got slotted for seventeen years, though. A good chunk of them in Pentridge. The old Bluestone College, as they say. He was in H Division for most of his sentence. "Hell Division", as we liked to call it. The worst of the worst.'

A bead of sweat runs down my chest.

'I'll be in touch, Tom. But until then, be careful.'

Five

I wake early, before the sun has fully risen. I make myself a coffee, stand in the kitchen in the half-light. I eat cold baked beans straight from the can.

The side door opens, heavy footsteps.

Cyril comes into the kitchen, takes off his coat. He gets a mug from the cupboard without saying a word.

I put the can down on the bench.

'Morning,' I say.

He nods. 'Good weekend?'

Had a visit from Neville. I told him about the bodies. Also heard you murdered a hitchhiker, then named your dog after her.

'Pretty quiet,' I say.

'Any visitors?'

I look out the window, try not to meet his gaze.

'A few around. No Lina today?'

Lina. Lina Fischer. All chopped up in a suitcase.

He refills the kettle. 'Rostered day off.'

I clench my jaw, do my best to act normally.

'What's on for today?'

He shrugs. 'Probably just some weeding, maybe cut some grass. I'll figure it out once I've had a coffee. No burials this week, thank Christ.'

We sit at either end of the bench. After a minute or two, the roller door slides up.

It's Seamus. He keeps his eyes down.

'Morning,' I say.

He doesn't answer, wheels his bike in against the shed wall.

The phone rings and it makes me jump.

'You get it,' Cyril says.

Seamus takes off his helmet, picks up the phone.

'Yep? Yeah, righto. I'll just get him.' He eyes Cyril, holds out the phone. 'It's Krystal. Says she needs to talk to you pretty urgently.'

My breath catches in my throat.

Cyril puts his mug down on the bench, lets out a sigh.

'Ah for fuck's sake. It never ends.'

He takes the phone, forces a smile.

'Morning, my sweetheart.'

He falls silent, glances at me, then Seamus.

'Yeah, they're both here.'

He turns his back, faces the wall. My hand starts to tremble.

'Fair dinkum?'

Seamus heads into the kitchen. Cyril picks up a pen, writes something on his wrist.

'Yep, I got it. We'll get it done asap. Yeah, I know. I'll come see you after.'

He hangs up the phone, lets out a long sigh. He turns and looks at me. I try to read his expression, but he gives me nothing.

Seamus comes back from the kitchen, carrying a coffee.

'What did she want?' he says.

'We've got a burial this week after all. Day after tomorrow.'

'Jesus, why such short notice?'

'Fuck knows,' he says. 'Anyway, we've got time.'

'Existing grave, or new?'

'New one.'

Seamus sips his coffee. 'Whereabouts?'

'Catholic section. Over near the west gate, beside the new mausoleum. Should be pretty straightforward, just a single.' He gives me a look, then Seamus. 'Actually, me and you might just handle it ourselves.'

'You don't want any help?' I say.

He shakes his head. 'You can make yourself useful elsewhere. Krystal says it's looking pretty dire down in the north-west corner. She says it's visible from outside, people walking past with dogs and whatnot, so it'd be good to clean up the weeds. Not good for business, you know.'

I nod. 'Fair enough.'

Seamus and Cyril finish their coffees in silence.

•

The weeds aren't as bad as Krystal made out. There are definitely far worse sections. It might be visible from out on Macpherson Street, but only just.

The sun is already getting warm, and the narrow straps of the backpack are cutting into my shoulders. After finishing a couple of rows, I decide to take a breather.

I sit down on the edge of one of the graves. It belongs to Josef Finkelstein, who died in 1952. His headstone is badly askew. The long, flat ledger stone that lies over the grave has broken in half, exposing the shadowy void beneath.

After a few minutes, I continue down the row, spraying the Round-Up here and there, but my thoughts drift elsewhere.

I asked Neville to hold off on the story for a few days, but maybe he couldn't. Maybe that's what Krystal needed to talk to Cyril about so urgently, not just the new burial.

If they know I've told Neville, I need to get out of here now. There's no telling what Cyril might do.

But maybe Neville couldn't get the idea past his editor, or legal. Another writer could be doing the article, the one with the headline.

I'm probably being paranoid. I'll buy a newspaper tomorrow, just to be sure.

Still, there was something strange in the way Cyril looked at Seamus. Some kind of message passed wordlessly between them.

It's still two days until I said I'd call Lucy, but I wish I could speak to her now. Either way, I'll book the bus trip on Wednesday. Even if she gets cold feet and doesn't want to see me, I can't stick around here.

Better to get out beforehand.

I look up from my spraying, spot a woman up ahead. She's standing in front of a grave, hands on her hips. She looks in her late forties, wearing a bright floral dress. I give her some space, move into the next row.

'Hello,' she says.

I look at her and nod. 'Morning.'

'You work here?'

I stop spraying. 'Yeah.'

She brushes a few stray hairs away from her face.

'Must be fascinating, working in a place like this. In a morbid kind of way. Probably a bit depressing at times.'

'I haven't been here that long.'

She nods. 'I haven't seen you before, so that figures. My name's Jessica.'

'Tom.'

'It's nice to meet you.' She gestures toward the grave. 'This is my husband, Geoffrey.'

Geoffrey Markov
Beloved husband to Jessica
1–5–1964 to 8–12–2011
'I am the thousand winds that blow
I am the diamond glints in snow
I am the sunlight on ripened grain
I am the gentle autumn rain'

'I'm sorry,' I say.

She nods.

'It was completely out of the blue. He was getting dressed after having a shower, and I heard this heavy thump in the bedroom. I found him there on the floor, unconscious. So I ran out into the street, screaming for help. I didn't know what else to do.

'Someone called an ambulance, and they tried to revive him. I watched them pump his chest, but it didn't help. I can never get the image out of my mind, you know? It's what I wake up to every day. All the colour, the life in him, it just drained from his face.'

'Must've been a terrible shock.'

She nods. 'I know they say it's better to have loved and lost, that old cliché. But I'm not so sure anymore. And I still see him sometimes. I mean, I know he's gone, but sometimes I see him around the house. Even here, standing there behind the grave. I just wish I could have done something. If I'd known first aid, or gotten help more quickly.'

'I'm sure you did your best.'

She shakes her head. 'It wasn't good enough, though, was it?'

I'm not sure what to say.

'Losing someone you love makes you realise what's important. Only problem is, it's always too late.'

I look ahead, down the row.

'I don't want to keep you,' she says.

I nod. 'I'd better get back to it. And again, I'm sorry about your husband.'

She looks at me, her eyes on the verge of tears.

'We all know it's coming, one way or another. But the knowing doesn't make it any easier.'

•

After an hour or so, I decide to call it quits. I figure I've done enough to keep Cyril and Krystal happy.

I take the Round-Up back to the shed, but Cyril and Seamus aren't back yet. I decide to pick up my pay from the office. I take the scenic route, via First Avenue.

The sun is out from behind the clouds, and I feel better than I have for a while. It feels good to have a plan, to have made a decision. Whatever happens with Neville and the article, I'll be out of here soon enough.

No-one is there when I get to the office. I ring the bell on the counter, hear movement out back. It's maybe a minute before Krystal appears.

She smiles brightly.

'What brings you here? Business or pleasure?'

'Just came to get my pay.'

'Oh, that's a shame. You're gonna sort that bank account, right?'

'Next week, definitely. By the way, I finished that weeding you asked for.'

She frowns. 'Weeding?'

'The north-west corner? Cyril told me you wanted it done.'

'Oh yeah, that's right. We always need to look presentable, don't we? Back in a tick.'

She heads out back, returns after a minute or two with a yellow envelope.

'Thanks.'

'No worries. I'm afraid I haven't got much time to chat today, bit of work to do.'

'Righto.'

She arches an eyebrow. 'By the way, has that journo been in touch again? Neville, wasn't it?

I try my best to hold her gaze.

'Nah, I think he must've cooled on the whole idea.'

She nods. 'That's good. But if he comes by here again, I'll make sure he goes away. Cyril said that's what you want, right?'

'Yep, that'd be great.'

She tilts her head. 'Was there something else?'

'Nah, I'll let you get back to it.'

She taps her nails on the counter. 'Just don't forget to sort that bank account. This is the last time I'm paying you cash, okay?'

'Understood.'

•

It's late afternoon by the time Seamus and Cyril get back to the shed. Seamus carries a shovel, Cyril an extendable saw.

'What took so long?' I say. 'I thought it was just a single.'

'Yeah, but it turned out to be a killer,' Cyril says. 'Some big roots from an elm on the other side of the fence. We could've used your help, actually.' He hooks the saw on the wall. 'Did you get that weeding done?'

'Yeah.'

He nods. 'Good stuff. Me and Seamus are knackered, so we're gonna call it a day. Catch you tomorrow, yep?'

'Righto.'

Seamus gets his bike from against the wall.

'See you, Seamus,' I say.

He looks at me, but doesn't answer. He turns and heads out through the roller door.

Cyril shakes his head. 'Don't mind him, mate. In a foul mood. He had a flutter on the weekend, then chased his losses. Blew pretty much all of that cash. Some people never learn, right? It doesn't matter what you do.'

'Right.'

He smiles, the silver glistens in his teeth.

'I'll see you tomorrow, Tom. Bright and early.'

•

That night, a dream.

I'm walking somewhere.

Down a narrow path.

At its end, there's a timber fence.

A gateway.

I walk toward it, open the gate.

I've been here before, I'm sure of it.

I go through the gate, then down a long driveway beside a weatherboard house. I come out into a dusty backyard.

It looks familiar, but different.

There's a trampoline tipped on its side. A steel bin turned upside down.

The boy is there.

He throws me the ball.

'I'll bat first this time,' he says. 'One hand, one bounce, but no LBW. If you hit the house on the full, you're out. Six and out if you hit it over the fence. You're West Indies, I'm Australia.'

I go back to my run-up, a little way up the driveway. The sun is warm, and there's a gentle breeze at my back. The smell of honeysuckle, stronger now. Soft and sweet, like vanilla.

He marks his crease, taps his bat on the ground.

'You're ready?' I say.

'Yep. But remember, you can't get out first ball.'

'Yeah, I know.'

I run in, the ball in my hand, the tape up one side. The boy steps forward, drives crisply through the off-side.

'That's four,' he says.

I pick up the ball, go back to my run-up. I can smell something cooking. My stomach rumbles. Out on the back veranda, a woman comes out. She's got an apron on, hands on her hips.

'You boys happy with spaghetti?'

'Yep,' I say.

She smiles. 'I'm glad you've come home, Fabri. I've been waiting so long. I hope you're hungry.'

I run in and bowl again.

The sun beats down, the day stretches out ahead of us.

And somehow, it doesn't matter if I win or lose.

Or what happens next.

Because that moment, that summer, it might just go on forever.

I wake around midnight to the cool darkness of the shed. I try to hold on to the feeling from the dream, its bright sunlight and warmth. Slowly, it begins to fade.

I go to the kitchen and pour myself a glass of milk. I look out through the window, across the cemetery and out toward Lygon Street. The graves scattered and broken like jagged teeth.

In the corner of my eye, there's movement.

I look down Fourteenth Avenue, the dark road snaking through the eastern side.

There's someone there, on the side of the road. A dark shape moving between the graves.

I put down my glass.

I pull on my jeans, my boots. I go out through the side door.

I walk down the road. There's a cool breeze blowing from the south, the hint of winter approaching. I wish I'd brought my jacket.

I go slowly, carefully.

I'm downwind, but I don't want them to hear me.

Maybe they snuck in through one of the gaps in the fence. Probably just some kid on a dare. Or maybe someone sleeping rough.

Then, I see him.

He's up ahead, standing perfectly still in the middle of the road. He's looking toward me.

I hold my breath.

I move slowly forward.

He holds my gaze, his thick tail curling left and right.

I stop, let out a long, slow breath.

I close my eyes.

The smell of my father's coat, the gun at his side.

The air, crisp and cool on my skin.

He is very wise, the fox.

I open my eyes.

The fox turns, slips silently between the graves.

Disappears into the night.

I reach into my pocket, feel for my lucky charm. The rabbit's foot, dry and bony in my fingers. I give it a squeeze.

I cross my arms to the cold.

The fox we saw all those years ago.

He knew he was in danger.

He knew to escape.

I turn and walk slowly back up Fourteenth Avenue. The road curves ahead like a river. The wind from the south is stronger now, the cold cuts through my shirt. My mind starts to race.

I need to leave tonight, just to be safe.

Catch the next bus to Brisbane.

The road arches toward the fence on the Macpherson Street side, the shed and the gate beyond.

I cross my arms to the cold, walk more quickly. At North Avenue, I turn right and head toward the shed.

Someone's there.

They're moving slowly along the path at the side of the shed. They're carrying something. It's hard to tell from here, but it looks like some kind of tool. Could be a pickaxe.

I crouch down behind a tall headstone. I look around its edge and watch them go closer to the side door.

They pause, lower the pickaxe at their side. Against the door, I see their silhouette more clearly. A man, short and stocky.

Cyril.

He opens the door ever so slowly, lifts his arm. And it's then I see.

It isn't a pickaxe.

It's a gun.

The weeding they got me to do, the grave they dug in the Catholic section.

It's meant for me.

My heart beats hard in my chest.

Cyril goes inside the shed, flicks on the light. After a few seconds, he comes back and stops just outside the doorway. I crouch down lower behind the headstone, but I can't stay here.

I'm too close.

He'll find me for sure.

A beam of torchlight flashes across the road, then up a row of graves just a few metres away.

I have to run.

It's my only chance.

I stand up and bolt down the path, back toward Fourteenth Avenue. At the edge of the road my boot catches on the gutter, pitching me forward onto the bitumen.

Pain shoots up my right leg, blood in my mouth.

The torchlight comes closer. Footsteps coming fast down the road. As the beam of light comes nearer, the footsteps slow.

A few metres away there's an old grave, tilted badly askew. The long, flat ledger stone that sits atop the grave is broken, the bottom third missing.

It's my only hope.

I crawl inside the grave as quickly as I can, then slide underneath the broken stone. The earth beneath it, subsided, is cool on my skin. I pull my knees in tight, close to my chest.

I reach into my pocket, give the rabbit's foot a squeeze.

Footsteps coming closer now.

I close my eyes and listen to the wind through the trees.

The footsteps stop.

A cold weight fills my stomach, my chest.

'I know you're around here, mate. Saw you go arse over tit.'

His voice, so close.

'Best come out and end things with some dignity, yeah? Better to die on your feet than live on your knees, as they say.'

I hold my breath, grip the rabbit's foot tight.

'You know, I had a real good feeling about you, Tom. But I guess my instincts were off this time. Between you and Kev, I must be getting rusty. He's another one I had to dispatch. Real shame, it was. I planted that dickhead just a few rows from here. He's got a nun on top of him, actually. Quite a privilege – not many blokes could say they've ever had that. Sweet Sister Eleanor.'

He's closer now, maybe a few metres away. I keep as still as I can, slow my breathing.

'I'm big on loyalty, you see. And giving people a second chance. Thing is, I made a few mistakes when I was young, just like you. When I went inside, no-one wanted to know me.

I was *persona non grata*, as they say. But eventually, some people accepted me. I never forgot about that. But I had to repay that trust, you know?'

A bright flash of torchlight inside my grave, beneath the ledger stone, then darkness.

'Look, in some ways, I don't blame you. For telling that journo, I mean. I'm not sure you had much choice. After all, life is just cause and effect, when you boil it down. That's pretty much all that exists in the universe. I tried to explain that to you once, but I guess it didn't sink in.'

A twisting feeling in my stomach, my chest.

'Your life and my life have always been headed for this moment. But neither of us knew it. There's really nothing we could've done. We're just biological machines, interacting with an environment we can't control. Same as everyone else. We think we have control over what happens, but it's an illusion. Think about it. You couldn't stop that Ronnie bloke fucking your mate, could you? And that's what led to everything that followed.'

From somewhere deep in the trees, I hear a currawong call.

Then, I hear the bolt of the rifle slide back and forth.

'No-one wants the music to stop, Tom. But it has to. It's the same for all of us.'

I dig my fingers into the earth, squeeze as tight as I can.

His footsteps move slowly past the grave.

He mustn't have seen me.

I twist my body around and slowly lift my head through the gap in the ledger stone.

He's maybe five metres away, standing on the road with his back to me, turning the torch left and right.

If I stay here, he'll find me.

If I stay here, I'll die.

I climb out from under the ledger stone as quietly as I can. I stay low, crawling along the concrete path on my hands and knees.

Once I get to the road, I run.

The torch beam flashes across my path, but I can't stop now.

A gunshot rings out, then another.

I keep running down Fourteenth Avenue, darting left and right, until I get to the fence at Lygon Street. A row of thick shrubs line the edge of the cemetery. I crouch between the shrubs and the fence, try to keep out of sight.

Another gunshot. The bullet pings against the fence, just above my head.

I get down on all fours and crawl until I see what I'm looking for. A gap in the fence, where an iron post broke and was never replaced.

I look back toward the torchlight coming fast down the road. I reach into my pocket. I take out the rabbit's foot, my lucky charm. I give it a squeeze.

I climb through the gap, onto the footpath outside.

I look back one last time, take a deep and ragged breath in and out. The torchlight's coming closer.

I turn and run to the other side of the street, down a darkened laneway, and disappear into the night.

Three Days Later

GRAVE DISCOVERY: VIGILANTE KILLER RELEASED

By Neville Barton

A former prisoner, convicted for one of Victoria's most notorious crimes, has been working as a gravedigger in the Melbourne General Cemetery.

Fabrizio Morressi served nine years for being an accessory to the 1995 killing of convicted child sex offender, Ronald Bellamy. Mr Morressi was found to have disposed of Mr Bellamy's remains in a manner the sentencing judge described as 'frightening'. The murderer, Ben Carver, committed suicide shortly after he was sentenced.

Mr Carver was 18 years of age at the time of his offence, attacking Mr Bellamy with a rock at an isolated property near Stawell, in western Victoria. Mr Morressi, also 18, witnessed the murder, then dismembered and disposed of Mr Bellamy's body in an act described as 'utter savagery'.

The trial heard that Mr Bellamy was alleged to have sexually abused Mr Carver over a number of years.

Mr Bellamy's remains were not discovered until eleven years after his murder, concealed in a wheelie bin in the Wimmera River.

After completing his sentence last month, Mr Morressi, who has since changed his name, found employment at the cemetery. He told *The Argus* that he's now hopeful he can put his crime behind him.

'It was a long time ago. When we were kids, things were different. We just didn't know.'

Mr Morressi was reluctant to speak about Mr Bellamy's abuse of his friend, describing it as 'too painful.'

'There was something weird about him. Like what he said didn't really match up with what he was thinking. I wish I could've told someone [about the abuse]. Ben was my best mate.'

In recent years, Mr Morressi has received support online from victims of crime groups. Some consider him a hero for helping his friend, blaming the justice system for its failure to protect the most vulnerable.

Meanwhile, the CEO of Jesuit Social Services, Yvette Goldie, said Mr Morressi's release highlights the difficulties many prisoners face when returning to the community.

'A significant proportion find themselves without housing and social supports and often reoffend. It's a terrible cycle, and not enough is being done to address the disadvantage that leads to crime. Governments spend too much money putting ambulances at the bottom of cliffs instead of fixing the fence at the top.'

When contacted by *The Argus* about Mr Morressi's employment, Melbourne General Cemetery issued a statement.

'Mr Morressi was engaged on a trial basis but is now pursuing other opportunities. He was a reliable and diligent worker and we wish him the very best.'

The Argus sought further comment from Mr Morressi but was unable to reach him before publication.

Three Weeks Later

CEMETERY SCANDAL: TRIO ARRESTED OVER ILLEGAL BURIALS

By Neville Barton

Three cemetery employees have been arrested and charged in relation to alleged illegal burials at the Melbourne General Cemetery.

Krystal McAlpine, 38, Cyril Jacka, 54, and Seamus Doherty, 32, were remanded in custody ahead of a committal hearing next month.

Following an anonymous tip-off, Victoria Police detectives recently ordered a number of exhumations at the cemetery. Unidentified human remains were discovered beneath two legitimate burials. Police suspect the remains are connected to organised crime, although investigations are continuing. The families of those buried above the remains are not thought to have any connection to the illegal burials.

It is believed that further charges are likely to be laid against the employees, but police are appealing to the public for information. A police source confirmed that additional exhumations may be ordered in the coming weeks.

The arrests follow last month's report in *The Argus* of the cemetery's hiring of Fabrizio Morressi, who served a nine-year sentence for his involvement in the 1995 murder and mutilation of notorious paedophile, Ronald Bellamy.

Mr Morressi, who changed his name to Tom Blackburn while in prison, recently resigned his position at the cemetery and is thought to have fled interstate. Police believe he can assist them with their inquiries.

Anyone with information is urged to contact Crime Stoppers on 1800 333 000.

Acknowledgements

My deepest thanks to my publisher, Vanessa Radnidge for her invaluable insights and support. Thanks also to my agent, Gaby Naher, for her enthusiasm and advice.

As with all my books, I'm indebted to Deonie Fiford for her exceptional editorial expertise. I'm also especially grateful to Annie Zhang and Winnie Dunn for their attention to every detail. In addition, my thanks to my publicist, Madison Garratt, and the talented team at Hachette Australia who continue to champion new Australian writing.

Needless to say, the events depicted in this novel are entirely fictional and in no way reflect upon the essential work of cemetery employees. In this respect, sincere thanks to Charlotte Haycock and Mark Boyall from the Greater Metropolitan Cemeteries Trust for their generosity and patience. Any errors in the technical descriptions of grave digging and burials are entirely my own. Thanks also to Roy Brandi who double-checked the accuracy of my Italian dialogue.

This book was written with the assistance of a Creative Australia grant, which gave me precious time to write. I also acknowledge the work of biological scientist Robert Sapolsky, whose books *Determined: Life Without Free Will* and *Behave* were invaluable guides to the complexity of free-will debates. His thinking has changed how I see the world, and my place in it. Likewise, Peter Singer's *Animal Liberation Now* helped my research and shifted my beliefs. I'm also thankful to Don Chambers for his book *The Melbourne General Cemetery*, which deepened my knowledge of its history.

The voice and music of Thom Yorke and Radiohead have been an essential thread in the creative process for each of my books. Thank you for sharing your gift with the world.

My heartfelt thanks to Georgia and Bubbles for your love and companionship. Writing novels can sometimes be a lonely pursuit, but it never feels that way.

Lastly, this book is dedicated to the memory of our staffy, Millie, who we love beyond measure. We will always miss you.

Discover how Tom's story begins in

Wimmera

Prologue

Dad told them never to cross the highway.

But the dam hadn't been much good that day. It was a green dam and Jed told Danny there were no yabbies in green dams, only fish if you're lucky. Yabbies were only in muddy dams. But Danny, as usual, reckoned he knew better.

They caught nothing, so Jed got bored and reckoned they should go to the river, just for a look. But they had to cross the highway to get there.

'What if Dad finds out?' Danny said.

Jed shrugged. 'How would he?'

They left the nets at the dam and Jed pushed down the lower lines of the fence with his foot so Danny could climb through without getting scratched by the barbed wire.

A long truck, belting north toward town, howled its horn as it tore past, destined for the abattoir. The smell of sheep shit and oily wool lingered, as Jed and Danny slid down the steep, stony embankment to the edge of the highway.

Jed was a good foot taller than Danny and could see down the road until it curved away to the west. To the east of the curve was a flat, yellow patchwork of paddocks that disappeared in a shimmer below the stony face of the Grampians, looming like a tidal wave at the horizon.

Above the range, blue-black clouds billowed and ruptured, and a grey veil descended across the mountains. The wind shifted quickly from the southwest to a cooler southerly, and Jed could tell the weather was coming soon. He could smell it, like the start of rain falling on a hot road. Like wet cement.

Then, without warning, Danny took off across the highway. Jed called out for him to stop, but his voice was lost in the wind as Danny disappeared down the slope on the other side.

The river. *Shit.* Danny couldn't swim.

Jed heard the nearing rumble of another truck, so he ran while he had the chance. The wind blew at him, willing him back. But he was a good runner and he pushed against it, the highway smooth and warm under his bare feet. He made it to the dry grassy edge, eyes watering and chest heaving. The truck's horn blasted as it passed.

He couldn't see Danny anywhere.

'Danny!' he yelled. Across a lazy field of long yellow weeds, a tall row of eucalypts swayed as the air whooshed through their branches. Just past those trees, he knew the river ran deep and strong.

'Danny!' The wind ripped his calls away and he could hear the coming thunder of another truck headed west.

Jed ran through the weeds and toward the trees, his legs bouncing on the dumb earth like rubber. He imagined telling his mum, trying to explain, but she'd never believe him. For certain, his dad would beat the living shit out of him, probably break some bones – maybe even kill him.

He would have to run away, go live in the bush somewhere, or the city.

He could never go back home.

'Danny!' he screamed. Startled, a cluster of sulphur-crested cockatoos erupted from the high branches of the eucalypts, squawking and screeching, their pure white feathers stark against the blackening sky.

The truck roared past behind him and, in the quiet after, Jed could hear the river surge, hidden deep within the trees and scrub.

* * *

As he first caught sight of water, flowing fast beyond a row of trees and thick shrubbery, the wind suddenly relented. He called out again, his voice broken and throat raw. Then, near the river, from behind a prickle bush, his brother stepped into view, with eyes wide and cheeks flushed red.

Jed felt a march of hot anger rise in his chest.

'You'll pay for that,' he said. 'You wait til later.'

Danny smiled. 'But I found something. Quick, come look!'

Jed followed him down to the river's edge, to where an ancient ghost gum had fallen into purpose, forming a long bridge across the water, its thick roots upended by rain, the river and time.

'There!' Danny pointed.

'Big deal,' Jed shrugged. 'A tree fell down.' He looked up at the sky closing in – for certain, they'd be riding home wet and cold. Danny screwed up his face and pointed again.

'Nah, look properly! Under the tree. It's stuck.'

Jed looked at the dead tree, the black rush beneath and the gathering yellow foam until he saw what Danny was pointing at – a green wheelie bin, wedged under the middle of the trunk, with water streaming along its sides.

'It's a rubbish bin,' Jed said. 'So what?'

Danny's face dropped. But Jed was intrigued. What was a town bin doing way out here?

He moved closer to the river, stepping through the low branches and over rocks to the soft earth at the water's edge.

He took hold of a root, a long dead artery, and leaned over the river, as close as he could without getting wet.

Rain began to fall through the canopy of eucalypts, but Jed wasn't thinking about that now. He climbed aboard the slippery trunk and moved closer, gripping a slick flex of branches as he stepped slowly across the bridge.

Danny watched from the riverbank. 'Be careful,' he said. But the rain was falling heavily and Jed couldn't hear a word.

As he got closer to the middle of the river, Jed thought he could see bolts screwed into the top of the bin. There were a lot of them, all around the edge of the lid.

It looked like someone wanted it closed up really tight. Like they didn't want it ever to be opened.

Like they didn't want what was in there to ever come out.

One

Ben saw the ambulance up the street when he was coming home from footy training, but he didn't think that much of it. When he got inside, his mum and dad were quiet, looking at the telly. *The Wonder Years* was on, but the sound was turned off. Then the phone rang and his mum ran to it, almost like she knew it was coming.

* * *

At dinnertime, his dad put on the black-and-white telly in the kitchen. *The A-Team* was on and Hannibal and Murdock were making some sort of catapult to help them escape from prison. They were using a bed frame, steel springs and even the bed sheets to make it. They had tools though, which really didn't make sense if they were supposed to be in prison.

Mum and Dad were both still quiet and Ben tried to think of something to say, so he told them about the ambulance up the road. Dad stopped chewing, looked at Mum and said, 'Ah yeah.' Then he went back to his chops and *The A-Team*. Mum didn't say anything.

* * *

After dinner, Mum served dessert, which was weird because they only ever had dessert on Sundays if they sat in the special room. In the special room they would sometimes have chocolate mousse with chopped-up nuts on top, especially if guests came over. Even with chocolate mousse, Ben didn't like the special room because it didn't have a telly in it, and the chairs were uncomfortable.

This time though, they were in the kitchen and there was no chocolate mousse. It was just Neapolitan ice-cream, but only the vanilla and strawberry were left. Ben never understood why his mum didn't just buy chocolate, but he never asked about it.

Dad went back to the couch and turned on the big telly, but Mum sat there at the kitchen table and watched Ben eat the ice-cream until he was finished. Then, after he'd licked all the melted bits at the bottom of the bowl, she told him that Daisy was dead. She had hanged herself on the clothesline.

No one said anything else after that.

* * *

Daisy Wolfe was fourteen, three years older than Ben, and they got on the same bus at the same stop. She never talked to anyone much, just chewed gum and listened to her Walkman.

One time, this total psycho grade six kid, Tom Joiner, was gonna bash Ben behind the bus shelter for no reason at all. But Daisy found out, grabbed hold of him and choked him in a headlock til he cried. She was pretty tough for a girl. And Ben kind of loved her a bit after that, though never told anyone.

He wondered why she'd done it, why she hanged herself. Maybe she was failing at high school or something. Or maybe the kids were teasing her. He didn't reckon it would be that, but. She was pretty good looking. 'Very popular with the boys' – that's what his mum said.

She must have been upset about something though. Ben wondered why she didn't just run away. That's what he would do if things ever got really bad. He'd never hang himself, no way. And definitely not in the backyard where his mum would find him.

He tried to imagine Daisy's body hanging from that old steel clothesline, creaking as it shifted in the wind. He could see her dark eyes and her legs, perfectly white, swinging in the air.

Then the wind would blow harder, the clothesline would creak, and her summer school dress ripple as the shit and piss slid down those smooth, creamy legs. He knew about the shit and piss because Fab had told him that's what happens. And Fab's cousin, Marco, had told him about it. Marco was eighteen and from Melbourne, and he knew about things like that, so Fab said it must be true.

Ben imagined that's how Daisy's younger brother, Joe, would have found her, with the shit and piss running down her legs. Just before she did it, she'd given Joe fifty cents to buy mixed lollies from the milk bar. He'd bought raspberry jubes, jelly teeth and a 'Big Boss' cigar. The milk bar was opposite the footy oval and Ben had seen him walking past, showing off with his cigar. Joe didn't know then that Ben and Fab had smashed his cubbyhouse at the block over the back. And he didn't know the real reason Daisy had given him fifty cents.

Ben heard his mum say that Joe had tried to wake Daisy up. That he got hold of her legs, tried to lift her, and was screaming at her to stop mucking around and just wake up. That's how Mrs Pickering, who lived next door, found out – she heard Joe crying like she'd never heard before. She called the ambulance and all that, but it was way too late.

And Mum said that Joe would never recover. But Ben didn't really know what she meant by that.

* * *

They buried Daisy quick. That's what Ben's dad said, that it was really quick. Mum said, quietly, they were doing it quick because of what she did. Ben wondered if that was because she'd start rotting sooner than normal, but he thought he better not ask.

The funeral was just a couple of days later, a Saturday. It was the only time Ben had ever seen his dad in a suit. It was navy blue and it made him look like the prime minister, but smaller and with brown hair. Mum even made him put a tie on. She said it was the first time he'd worn one since their wedding day, but he hadn't needed to tie that one up. So Mum had to help him do it and it took ages.

After she got Dad sorted, she cooked pancakes, then got all dressed up in a black skirt and jacket. She even had lipstick on, which made her look a bit fancy. But no one hardly said a word.

Ben was happy though. Mainly because he was allowed to stay home on his own, eat pancakes, and watch cartoons.

* * *

Two days after the funeral, Ben's dad offered to get rid of the clothesline and Daisy's parents agreed. He put his long blue overalls on and got the angle grinder from the shed. Ben wanted to go with him, but Mum said no. She said it wouldn't be right. Then his dad said he could come to the tip after, which was even better. They always picked up some good stuff at the tip, and Ben liked chucking rocks at the feral cats.

Dad said he'd be about an hour, but he came back from the Wolfes' nearly right away, his face all white. Mum asked what had happened and Dad said that Mrs Wolfe told him to *get the fuck away from it you cunt* in a voice like he'd never heard from a woman.

So the clothesline stayed. They didn't go to the tip. And the Wolfes left town.

* * *

It was three months later that the new neighbour moved in.

'A Statesman De Ville,' his dad said, without shifting his gaze from the telly. It was Friday, so he was drinking a big bottle of beer without a glass. 'Nice car. Must be on good money.' Mum didn't say much about it, but slipped a cork coaster on the table, while his dad took a swig. The cork ones were for family – she had fancy wooden ones with pictures of kangaroos that she used for guests in the special room.

The news was on – it was something about the World Expo that had been on in Queensland and how they reckoned it was the best ever. Ben pretended to watch, but it was boring and he was mainly thinking about the new neighbour.

Ben wondered if the neighbour knew about the clothesline and the last thing that hung there. The clothesline that rattled in the wind when he rode his bike past, like it was calling him closer. The clothesline with its cold steel poles, bolts and wires, spinning forever in that relentless southerly wind.

In the front yard, weeds had sprouted and the grass had grown long. And that nice, shiny blue car just sat there in the driveway.

ALSO BY MARK BRANDI

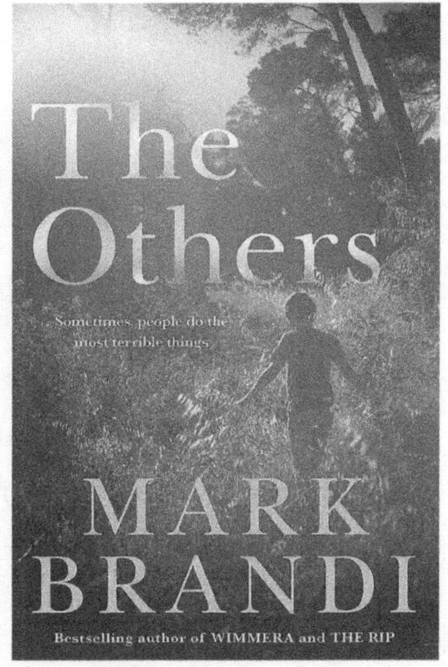

If you would like to find out more about Hachette Australia,
our authors, upcoming events and new releases, you can visit
our website or our social media channels:

hachette.com.au

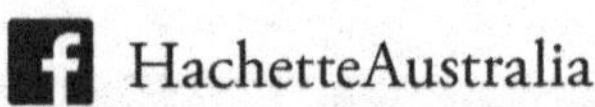 HachetteAustralia

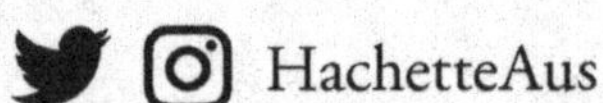 HachetteAus